THE PARTS LEFT OUT

Books by Thomas Ogden

Non-Fiction

Projective Identification and Psychotherapeutic Technique

The Matrix of the Mind: Object Relations and the Psychoanalytic Dialogue

The Primitive Edge of Experience

Subjects of Analysis

Reverie and Interpretation: Sensing Something Human

Conversations at the Frontier of Dreaming

This Art of Psychoanalysis: Dreaming Undreamt Dreams and Interrupted Cries

Rediscovering Psychoanalysis: Thinking and Dreaming, Learning and Forgetting

On Not Being Able to Dream: Selected Essays, 1994–2005 (available only in Hebrew)

Creative Readings: Essays on Seminal Analytic Works

The Analyst's Ear and the Critic's Eye: Rethinking Psychoanalysis and Literature (coauthored with Benjamin Ogden)

Fiction

The Parts Left Out

The Hands of Gravity and Chance

THE PARTS LEFT OUT
A Novel

Thomas H. Ogden

SPHINX

First published in 2014 by Karnac Books.

This new edition published in 2018 by Sphinx, an imprint of
Aeon Books
12 New College Parade
Finchley Road
London
NW3 5EP

British Library Cataloguing in Publication Data
A C.I.P. for this book is available from the British Library

ISBN-13: 978-1-91257-319-6

Typeset by V Publishing Solutions Pvt Ltd., Chennai, India

Printed in Great Britain

www.aeonbooks.co.uk

www.sphinxbooks.co.uk

For Warren Poland

The road out to the Bromfman farm in late August is no different from thousands of other roads to grain farms in Kansas—hard-baked dirt dusted with a fine powder of yellow clay that shifts almost imperceptibly with the slightest movement of the air. Randy Larsen was on his way to the farm in response to a call saying that someone had died out there. In Arwood County, one of the deputy sheriffs makes a routine inquiry into the circumstances of every death that occurs outside of County Hospital. These investigations most often turn into simple condolence calls. Randy supposed that one or another of the parents of Earl Bromfman and his wife—he couldn't remember her name—had died during a visit.

Randy knew Earl in high school when they were teammates on the football team. Every year some of the older players would razz the younger ones. Earl, a junior when Randy was a freshman, looked out for Randy when he first joined the team, something for which Randy remained grateful to this day. He remembered Earl as a "farm kid"—one of the children of farming families whose lives were unimaginable by those who grew up in town. Farm life was a life ruled by nature in ways the town kids could sense, but could never really grasp. Forces of immense power—hundreds of miles of black clouds of locusts that eclipse the sun; league after league of wheat blight that has the power to destroy an entire year's labor of thousands of people; farm animals' desolation after a stillbirth; the havoc wreaked by an aberrant early frost or a summer hail storm—all of this hovered silently over the farm kids, knowledge that nature has no enemies, nor does it have its favorites, knowledge that drew these children inward into terrible fear in the face of the limits of their parents' power to control their own fate, much less that of their children.

Earl, who recently turned thirty-six, was the third generation of Bromfman men to own and operate the family wheat farm. He was a large man with thinning, straight blond hair and penetrating blue eyes. His heft and deep resonant voice commanded respect that he didn't feel he deserved. Like many of the small farms in Arwood County, Earl's was struggling, in part because of a series of drought years, but mostly because the conglomerates, with their modern irrigation and transportation systems, were able to sell their harvest at a price lower than the small farmers could match. Earl took over the farm right after college, a decision welcomed by his father whose arthritis was growing worse each year, and by Earl's older brother and younger sister, who saw the farm as doomed.

Most of the small farms that remained were run by men whom Earl had known all his life. They had gone to the same school, the same church, they'd been in one another's house for one reason or another—delivering a casserole if someone was sick, picking up a tool or piece of machinery to borrow for a week or so. Earl had always been well liked, seen as a man who would back his friends and fight for their farms and their aging farm machinery as fiercely as he would fight for his own.

Earl's wife, Marta, a solemn woman of slight build, worked with Earl on the farm, along with one or two hired men who just seemed to appear as planting season approached and disappeared after harvest. Since the hard times began, Marta brought in some money by waitressing at the diner in town, part-time during the farming seasons, full-time in the winter. She was always pleasant to the customers and the others who worked at the diner, but she rarely smiled and never laughed. She did not talk about herself or her family, nor did she pry into anybody else's business; she arrived on time and left when her shift was over. It was hard to tell Marta's age because her face was a cobweb of wrinkles and creases etched into her skin by the sun and by her worries.

Marta had not wanted children, but had two. Warren and Melody, now eleven and fifteen, helped out with enough of the farm chores to save Earl the cost of hiring an extra hand. Melody taught Warren how to do increasingly difficult work as he got older. Having little time for anything but school and farm work, they were one another's best and only friend. The deep tie between them was evident to anyone who saw them together, though the nature of that bond was known only to the two of them.

The farmhouse on Earl's land was small, even by the standards of the neighboring farms. It consisted of three rooms—the kitchen, which occupied the entirety of the ground floor, and the two bedrooms on the upper floor—plus a small bathroom beneath the stairs. Earl and Marta slept in the larger of the two upstairs rooms, while Melody and Warren shared the other room. When Earl was a child, there were three beds in the smaller room to accommodate him and his brother and sister.

As a little boy, Warren had been very shy, trailing behind his mother from morning to night, never letting her out of his sight. Even as a two-year-old, he was awakened before sunrise by the sound of his parents dressing for the morning chores and would silently shadow his mother to the barn where she fed and watered the two plow horses. Warren would sit on the ground by one of the stalls sucking his thumb as he watched his mother work. His mouth and face would get streaked with a mixture of dirt, hay, and horse manure, which didn't seem to bother him. Marta viewed the boy's incessant need to be near her as a sign of weakness, a quality that did not bode well for him, for as she knew all too well, the weak do not fare well in this world.

What she found most repellant about Warren was his constant thumb sucking, and even worse, the delirious look on his face when he was doing it. He began sucking his thumb when he was only a few weeks old and seemed to do it more and more as he grew. He had his thumb constantly in his mouth not only in front of the family, but also, without a hint of embarrassment, in front of visitors to the farm and in school, even now at eleven, an age well past the time other children had given up the habit.

In recent years, whenever the schoolteacher, Miss Wells, spotted Marta in the diner, she made a point of telling her what a fine girl Melody was, almost a young woman now—so good-natured and eager to be of help. She would always add that Warren was a good boy, but he was a very quiet child who sat in the back row sucking his thumb, hardly joining in with the others in lessons or singing or sports. Every child is different—she'd learned that lesson time and time again during her many years of teaching—but one way or another they all seemed to grow up and come out fine. Marta would nod her head in agreement about how every child is different, even children from the same family, and how they each seem to find their own way, Lord only knows how. Inwardly, Marta cringed as Miss Wells talked about Warren, but you'd never know it from the expression on her face or the sound of her voice as she joined in with Miss Wells' praise of Melody and her confidence that Warren, like all the other children she had taught, would turn into a fine young man his parents would be proud of.

Miss Wells was right, Melody was a good girl, but it hadn't always been that way. When she was four, around the time Warren was born, she used to be a little terror, running around the house not listening to anything anyone

4

said. Slapping her bottom led to nothing but a full theatrical production of crying the likes of which you've never seen. It could make your head feel like it was splitting open, and cleaning all the stuff that came from her nose just added one more chore to the day. The only thing that worked with Melody was putting her in her room and telling her not to dare come out or she'd end up in the closet. Melody only needed to be latched in the closet a few times before she learned to behave, and she's been a very cooperative child ever since.

The next of Marta's encounters with Miss Wells occurred on a particularly hot and humid Saturday in the first week of August. Not only was every table in the diner filled, people were jammed together at the door, half inside and half outside the diner. With the door open, the air conditioning couldn't keep up with the heat pouring in from both the street and the kitchen. The back of Marta's uniform was soaked with perspiration as she tried to take the orders of the newly seated customers, serve the hot dishes that were piling up on the kitchen ledge, bring change to the customers who were impatiently waiting to leave, and bus the tables that were strewn with dirty glasses and dishes. Miss Wells had managed to corner Marta as she was holding a glass under the Coca-Cola spout of the beverage machine. Marta was able to excuse herself after a minute or so, but Miss Wells' report on Warren and Melody agitated her nonetheless.

That evening, as Warren was finishing clearing the table after supper, Marta, standing at the sink, her arms up to her elbows in the soapy water, said to Warren, "I saw Miss Wells today. She said you sit there in the back of the room sucking your thumb all day. You're eleven years old now and you ought to know better." Marta had learned how to deal with Melody when she was young, but she was at her wits' end with Warren. Even the closet hadn't worked with him. He was a willful boy. Marta's mother had never had to deal with anything like Warren, and even if she had, Marta hadn't spoken to her for many years and would never dream of asking her for advice about anything. Talking to Earl's mother, Flora, who died some years back, had never been of any use because she always sided with the children, which made Marta so angry that she had a hard time remaining civil.

On several occasions over the years Marta had gone to the drugstore intending to ask the druggist, Mr. Renkin, if he knew how to deal with thumb sucking in a child Warren's age, but each time her pride got the best of her and she couldn't get herself to talk to him, and instead bought a little something she didn't need so she wouldn't catch anyone's attention. She finally realized, not long after Warren's eleventh birthday, that she would never be able to bring herself to talk directly with Mr. Renkin, and that she would have an easier time dealing with the new part-time shopgirl, whose bright blue name tag with white lettering etched into it read "Jenny." Jenny, a slender red-haired girl, with large orange-brown freckles all over her face, couldn't have been more than a year or two out of high school. She was a type Marta had known in school and hadn't liked, the type with their hand up all the time, eager to show off. Marta would have much preferred to speak with an older woman with children of her own, who knew how difficult children could be.

Because the drugstore was right across the street from the diner, Marta could keep watch during her breaks and hurry over to the store when it was empty of customers. Trying to be as casual as possible, as if the problem she was having with Warren was commonplace, she asked Jenny in the friendliest and most motherly of tones she could muster, "Do you have anything people use to get children to keep their fingers out of their mouth?"

Jenny looked at Marta questioningly, not quite understanding what she was asking. "Do you mean something for a baby who puts everything into their mouth?"

"No, I mean something for an older child."

"An older child who does what with their fingers?"

"An older child who puts their thumb in their mouth."

"Oh, you mean an older child who still sucks their thumb. There was a girl in my class at school who did that till she was pretty old. It was sad and I used to feel bad for her. I'll ask Mr. Renkin what to do."

Jenny turned, walked behind the counter, and spoke under her breath to the druggist. Marta watched out of the corner of her eye. The way Jenny was whispering, and the grave expression on Mr. Renkin's face, made it look like the girl was asking about a treatment for syphilis, not a remedy for thumb sucking.

On returning, Jenny said to Marta, "Mr. Renkin told me to tell you not to worry. He said that this problem is not unusual and that children usually grow out of it, but some children have to be pushed. He suggests putting an ointment on the child's thumbs that tastes bad and smells bad, and makes the thumbs numb, which most children don't like and it gets them to stop. It will be ready in an hour or so."

As Marta walked back to the diner, she went over Mr. Renkin's words in her head several times, pleased to hear the words "some children have to be pushed." He seemed to understand what she was up against. She wouldn't tell Earl. There would be no need to trouble him with this. It was her job as a mother to handle these things. He probably wouldn't understand the harm that can be done if you let this kind of thing go on too long—he's often lackadaisical where the children are concerned, but that's a man's way, isn't it?

While it was Mr. Renkin's words that kept running through Marta's head, it was Jenny's voice saying the words that Marta was hearing. Jenny was just a girl, and a girl that age has no real experience with children, or with life for that matter. Nevertheless, the sound of Jenny's voice had a consoling effect on Marta. The girl treated Marta respectfully, as an elder—she called her Mrs. Bromfman after she talked to the pharmacist, who must have told her Marta's married name. Marta appreciated that.

During the remainder of the afternoon at the diner, business was slow. Marta checked the clock every ten minutes or so in anticipation of picking up the ointment. She rehearsed in her head the words she would use to tell Warren about the ointment that she'd be putting on his thumbs—actually he only sucked his right thumb, but he might start using the left one if the right one were no longer available to him. She imagined the expression on his face when she broke the news to him that the days of his embarrassing himself and the family were over. She would have to find a time and place in which she and the boy would not be interrupted by Earl or Melody. Probably taking him out back after the supper dishes were washed would be best. The last thing in the world she wanted was to have Earl or Melody spoil this plan that she had put so much time and effort into. It had not been easy for her, but since she was the only member of the family who took the matter seriously, it was left to her to tend to it.

Supper seemed interminable, but finally the table was cleared, the floor swept, and the dishes placed in the drying rack. Marta could see that Warren was about to slip away. She called after him, "Warren, I want a word with you." In his obedient but detached way, Warren turned and followed his mother out the back door to the expanse of sun-beaten, tire-marked dirt that stood between the house and the outhouse, which was now used only by the hired hands. An abandoned flatbed truck, an old thresher, and other broken farm machinery were silently going to rust.

"I saw Miss Wells the other day and she told me that you're a good boy, but that you stand out from the others because you have your thumb in your mouth most all the time. Is that so?"

Looking down at the ground, Warren said, "I guess."

"She said that you have to be encouraged to stop acting like that. Do you think that that would be a good idea and that you could use some help in doing that?"

"I don't know, yeah."

"Don't you feel embarrassed to be doing that at your age in front of everyone?"

"I guess so."

"I talked with Mr. Renkin at the drugstore and he said he had something that would help you break the habit. Do you want to see what it is?"

Still looking at the ground and making lines in the dry dirt with the toe of his right shoe, he quietly said, "All right."

"It's an ointment that goes on your thumbs to remind you what you're doing when you put your thumb in your mouth. After all this time, you don't know if your thumb's in your mouth or not. Do you think a reminder will help you remember that you're doing it so you can stop yourself?"

"I don't know. Maybe."

"I have the tube here and I'll put some on your thumbs so you can get started right away. There's no point in dawdling about it, is there?"

Marta carefully removed the tube of ointment from the paper bag Jenny had handed her only a few hours earlier. After squeezing some of the pale yellow ointment onto her forefinger, Marta looked at Warren who then held out both hands with his palms down. Marta took hold of his right forearm tightly and rubbed the ointment deep into the skin of his thumb, top and bottom all the way to the base. She then did the same with his other thumb. Warren put up no resistance. The acrid odor of the ointment irritated Marta's eyes, causing tears to run down her cheeks.

Warren retreated into the darkness of the house after the ointment was applied. Melody was in the bedroom she shared with Warren, sitting up on her bed reading a schoolbook, when Warren opened the door.

She looked up and asked, "What happened?"

"She put some stuff on my thumbs that smells and tastes bad."

"Does it hurt?"

"No, but my thumbs feel numb, as if they're blown up like a balloon when I touch something."

Melody quietly went to get a wet rag and some soap to try to get the ointment off of Warren's skin before it set in.

The next morning Warren fed and watered the horses and fed the chickens as he did each day before breakfast. A victory of sorts, Marta thought, when she saw him without his thumb in his mouth and that awful expression of self-satisfied contentment on his face. Weeks went by with new applications of ointment morning and night. The house was even quieter than usual, with only a few words spoken when something needed doing. The quiet was anything but peaceful. The air that the four of them breathed was suffused with the battle being waged between Marta and Warren.

Though just a boy, Warren was a match for his mother. He took her on in a way that neither Earl nor Melody ever dared. The battle between them appeared to be about his behavior—the thumb sucking that was so loathsome to Marta—but what was at stake was far greater than that habit. A life-and-death struggle was going on between them. At stake was his will, and hers. Neither of them had anything but their will to call their own. Marta, in her own mind, was neither a farmer nor a waitress, neither a wife nor a mother—she was a pale flame that refused to be extinguished. She *was* her refusal to have her will thwarted. Similarly, Warren, in his mind, was neither a son nor a schoolboy. He *was* his refusal to be extinguished by his mother.

In the midst of this period of intensified warfare, one morning, after Warren had completed his early morning chores, Marta spied Warren sitting behind the barn with his thumb in his mouth. Either he had trained himself to ignore the effects of the ointment, which was entirely possible for Warren, or he had found some way to get it off his fingers. It occurred to Marta that Warren might not have been caught unaware in his breach of her command; he might have been flaunting his victory over her. The effect of Marta's seeing the boy with his thumb in his mouth was felt by the whole family as piercingly as the report of a gun. Not a word had to be spoken. A radical change had occurred that seemed to affect the entire physical and mental world of the family, as if the intensity of the light from the sun had suddenly increased markedly, and the air had become far thinner than it had been. A change in Marta had been set in motion that no one in the world except Earl had seen before. Marta's response this time was not to seethe with rage as was her wont when Warren disobeyed. Instead, she sunk so deeply into herself that she no longer seemed to be living in the same house, or even the same world, as the other members of the family.

During this period, which lasted for several days, Marta repeatedly lost and regained her ability to put her thoughts into words for herself. When she was able to talk to herself about what she was feeling, she was aware that she was not simply consumed with bitterness or a hunger for revenge; what she felt was futility, not only in connection with her struggle with the boy, but also in connection with the growing realization that she would never escape the confines of the life fate had dealt her. As a student at the state university, she had met Earl, a boy whom she liked but didn't love—she still wasn't sure what the word *love* meant when she heard other people use it. Marta married him at twenty-one, had two children by the time she was twenty-five, and had lived her adult life as a farmer's wife, which was something she had sworn to herself she would never allow to happen. There were some women who didn't marry or have children, but they seemed stronger than she was. They could accept being an outsider, being looked on with pity, being seen as not really a woman.

Marta savaged herself for being so weak as to have ended up where she was.

During this series of days that all ran together in her mind, Marta found herself rushing across the street to the drugstore, this time not to ask for a further remedy—for she knew there wasn't one to be found there—but to say something to Jenny. As Marta opened the door to the pharmacy, she seemed different to Jenny—she was looking Jenny straight in the eye and was carrying herself with burning determination.

Marta firmly ushered Jenny toward the corner of the store farthest from where Mr. Renkin was working. "I have a few words to say to you, and if I don't say them now, I'm afraid I may never say them, so please hear me out. This will only take a minute or so. You're young now, and there's still a chance for you to make some decisions before they get made for you. You should know that when you marry and have children, the life that you had is taken from you. No, in truth, you give it away in agreeing to marry and have a family, but most women don't know that and don't really make a decision to have a family, they just go ahead and do it. It takes a very strong woman to decide not to marry and have children, and you may or may not be one of them, but I want you to make a decision about it before doing it because if you've really chosen that life, I think you will feel less bitter about the life you've given up."

Marta didn't wait for a reply. She hadn't intended to have a conversation, it was just something she had to say to this girl who had delivered a very private message to her in a way that had allowed her to preserve a little dignity. Marta left the drugstore with such quick steps that she seemed to leave a draft in her wake.

Marta was now living in a state of mind in which one does not consider; one is swept along in a torrent of action. She could feel the direction in which she was moving, but felt nothing about it except its imperative force. What was about to happen would happen regardless of any interference on anybody's part. Marta did not know the source of the idea that had taken hold of her—she was merely its agent, not its architect. The idea may have had its origins in something her mother or grandmother or even a friend had told her when she was a child, or in a conversation she overheard, or perhaps in a dream, or maybe it was a plan solely of her own making that had been spawned months or years ago which was now convulsively transforming itself from an imagining into something that could not be more real and could not be stopped.

TWO

Instead of returning to the diner as was her pattern after her previous visits to the drugstore, Marta made her way directly to the dry goods store. She selected a pair of leather work gloves and some leather shoelaces. The next thing she knew she was on the street again, and had no memory of who had been at the cash register or of having opened her purse to pay for her purchase. She looked at her hands to see if she was carrying a bag that contained work gloves and shoelaces, and if so, what sort of bag it was. She saw in her left hand a brown paper bag. She peered inside and saw the work gloves and laces that she had intended to buy, which reassured her that she was not losing her mind. Nonetheless she worried that she might have appeared strange or said something nonsensical, or worse yet, said something about why she was buying these things. She wondered if she was dreaming and would soon awaken to discover that her life was quite simple and conventional. What a gift that would be—but her life had never offered up gifts of that sort.

When Marta finally returned to the diner, she found that she'd been gone for over an hour. The remainder of the day held no significance except as a period of waiting before the main event began. This kind of waiting was familiar to Marta.

As a child, each day was a day of waiting for the main event, her father's return home at the end of the day. She had learned how to hold terror at bay while she waited. Of course things were different now—she was a grown woman with a husband and children, but somehow the feeling of that particular kind of waiting was still very much a part of her life.

At supper Earl said, "The weather report is for no rain this week, and probably very little for a few weeks."

A few minutes later: "Jeffers from across the way says his mare has come down with something. The vet's been out and says it's probably the flu. That'll spread like wildfire."

Earl didn't seem to be talking to anyone in particular, nor did he seem to expect a reply. Warren and Melody were silent, as they always were at supper, not looking at anything but the food on their plate. Marta was deep in thought.

Just before bedtime, Warren didn't seem surprised when his mother told him to go out back with her, nor did he show any response to the tan, leather work gloves that his mother took from the paper bag.

"Hold out your hands and I'll put these on you. It's for your own good. You can't go on being a baby instead of being like other boys your age."

Warren extended his arms, palms upward, fingers extended and spread apart, as if showing his mother that he wasn't hiding anything. After sliding his fingers into the gloves, which were far too big for him, Marta took two thick leather shoelaces from the bag and carefully tied them firmly around the sleeve of each glove. The laces were long, so they had to be wound around the wrists several times, which made them look much messier than Marta had envisioned. Warren was silent, keeping his eyes fixed on the dark line that the tops of the hills made against the evening sky behind his mother's head.

After all the earlier failed attempts at blocking Warren from sucking his thumb, Marta knew that she was up against an extraordinarily stubborn boy. He had ceased being her child, and she had ceased being his mother; he was an animal that she had to break, and she was a woman who could not rest until this task was done. She hadn't a clue how it had come to this—events seemed to have hurtled themselves forward, one upon the next, carrying her to this scene in which she was tying leather gloves on an eleven-year-old boy so tightly that she knew that if she misjudged only slightly, she could cut off the blood supply to his hands, causing them to become gangrenous, which would require amputation of his fingers, or perhaps the entirety of his hands—maybe that was the precipice toward which she was irresistibly drawn.

Warren neither cried nor pleaded.

The next morning Warren emerged from his room with the gloves on his hands and the leather laces knotted. He stood in front of his mother, silently asking her to remove the gloves so that he could change his clothes and do the chores he had to complete before breakfast. Marta untied the laces, pulled the gloves off the boy's hands, and carefully placed them in the bottom drawer of the wooden dresser to the right of the wood-burning stove. He then returned to his room to put on his work clothes as if nothing unusual had occurred.

This pattern was repeated for several days. One morning after Warren had dressed, he went out to the barn where his father and Melody were already at work. Before he stepped into the barn, he heard Melody imploring her father to stop her mother from treating Warren so cruelly. "She's insane, you know that. Why don't you stop her?"

Earl was at a loss for words. He eventually said, "It's not that easy. Your mother's pride has been hurt by Warren. She suffers when Warren embarrasses himself and her at school and in front of neighbors."

"She's tying him up in leather gloves and ropes. I can't bear to see it. I don't know how you can. I untie him after she goes to sleep and re-tie him in the morning."

Earl looked at her with his deep, sad eyes and said, "I know you do. That's the right thing to do."

"If you think that it's the right thing to do, why don't you do something yourself? Why don't you do the thing that's right?"

"I wish I could explain it to you, Melody, but I don't know how."

"I don't care what the explanations are, I only care that you do something. You're his father."

"You don't have to remind me of that," Earl replied. "I never forget, even if it looks like I do."

Warren watched silently from the door of the barn.

Marta was in the kitchen when the three returned from their chores. She sensed something had happened out there. It was as if she suddenly woke up to something that had been right in front of her all along. Marta said in a low, expression-less voice, "Come over here." There was no need for her to explain to whom she was talking. Warren walked over to her and held out his hands, palms down without her having to ask. Marta took his hands in hers one at a time and examined them closely. She was interested primarily in his right thumb. The skin of that thumb was still soft from having been in his mouth all night, and as significant were the depressions that his two lower front teeth had left in the skin on the top of the inner half of the thumb, tell-tale impressions that were all too familiar to Marta. She now knew for certain that Warren had slept with his right thumb in his mouth all night, and that Melody or Earl, or both of them, had removed the gloves and put them back on him in the morning. Warren turned and took his place at the kitchen table, his back to his mother.

Marta plunged into a rage the wildness of which neither Earl nor the children had ever seen. She shrieked and cried and beseeched God to tell her what she had done to deserve a child such as this most stubborn, hateful, self-centered boy who shames himself, her, and the family every day of his life.

She shouted at him, "I never wanted you. Do you know that?" Warren, still facing away from her, showed not the least surprise at what she had said.

Earl stepped toward Marta, but she retreated, screaming, "Get away from me, don't you dare touch me."

Earl said as quietly and calmly as he could, "Marta ... Marta, you've been a good mother to the boy, you've done right by him."

Stillness took hold of the room. That quiet, timeless moment before a hand grenade explodes. The sun had risen higher over the storage shed and was casting a slanted stream of bright light on the tabletop, before leaping to the far wall where it bleached the yellowing paint to a chalky white. The spell broke when Marta lifted her head and turned her gaze to Earl and Melody, who were standing between her and the table where Warren was seated. She lashed out, "The two of you have been in it with him from the start. I've gone through hell with him, and you have the gall to judge me and undo everything I've toiled to achieve."

Warren, still seated at the kitchen table with his back to what was happening, looked impassively into the glare from the windows.

In as gentle a voice as he could manage, Earl said, "We're not against you. We know you care for the boy and that you're doing your best to help him."

Marta paced back and forth along the wall against which the stove and sink stood, her eyes glazed over. Then, in what seemed like a single movement, she grabbed a knife from the top of the chest of drawers to the right of the stove, flew past Earl, took hold of Warren's right hand with her left and pressed it flat against the table in front of him, knocking to the floor his empty plate, cup, and fork. Leaning over his right shoulder, continuing to hold Warren's hand to the table, she raised her arm to stab the hand that so oppressed her. The boy did nothing to resist. Earl, emerging from momentary paralysis, lunged forward, grabbed her right arm above the elbow, and jerked Marta away from Warren. As Marta spun around in Earl's direction, the blade of the knife grazed Earl's shoulder. The rage in Marta's eyes seemed to grow all the more wild in the face of Earl's treachery. She staggered back away from Earl, regained her balance, and attempted another strike at the boy's hand, which was still outstretched on the table, fingers splayed as she had left them. Earl grabbed her forearm, this time far more forcefully, twisting her body away from the table so that they were face to face, with only inches between them. Earl, holding Marta's right arm tightly to her side, was taken by surprise by the enormous physical strength with which Marta wrenched her arm free of his grip, slicing the web of skin between his thumb and forefinger as she freed herself. He glanced at his hand, which was bleeding profusely, before looking up to find Marta's eyes glaring threateningly into his. She was once again standing erect, gathering herself for another attack on Warren. Earl retreated a stride, and then, with bended knees, hands to his side, exploded upward, driving his right shoulder into Marta's neck, knocking her into the air. She was thrown backward, her arms seeming to reach out to grab hold of something, her head hitting the floor before the rest of her body landed, the knife flying backward and then skittering across the floor toward the foot of the stairs to the second floor. And then nothing.

Marta's body lay motionless, her shoulders flat against the floor as if pinned by an invisible wrestler. What was most alarming was the way in which her head extended from her neck at an impossible angle, resembling the head of a broken doll tossed on a heap of refuse. Her arms and legs were sprawled every which way, signaling an absolute and final disconnection of body and soul.

Earl took a few tentative steps forward, knelt down beside Marta's head, and slowly slid his left hand under her upper back and his right hand under the base of her head. As he began to lift her toward a seated position, her head flopped sideways toward him. He reflexively extended his arms in fear before gently lowering her to the floor. The room was now silent in a way that was different from anything they had ever known. The air was thick with the moving motes of dust illuminated by the slanted sunlight beating in from the windows. Warren was still seated at the table, never having turned to look at what was happening behind him. Melody stood a few paces behind her father, looking down at him as he knelt next to the body.

After some time—none of them knew how long—Melody asked, "Is she dead?"

Earl, in a world of his own, did not hear the question. Melody took small steps in the direction of her mother. She couldn't see any movement in her mother's chest. A small pool of blood moved outward from where her mother's right ear was pressed to the floor.

Melody thought, it's my fault that this happened. I hated her. I don't want a mother. I never want to be one.

Earl thought, she hurt more than anyone, even more than the boy.

Warren looked directly into the sun until he had to close his eyes, seeing spots of every color dancing before him.

Melody broke the silence, "Don't we have to call someone?"

Earl hadn't thought that far ahead: it didn't feel real that he had killed his wife a few minutes—or was it hours?—earlier, and was now kneeling next to her dead body. What else was there to do but call the sheriff's department?

Randy Larsen, driving the cream-colored county sheriff's car with the green sheriff's insignia and motto painted on the side, arrived at the Bromfman farm less than an hour after Earl's call. When he pulled in next to Earl's pickup, Earl was outside waiting, a bandage on his right hand, wrapped awkwardly around his thumb and forefinger.

"Hey Earl, sorry to hear that someone died out here."

It felt to Earl that Randy was trying to be neighborly while leaving open the possibility that more than that would become necessary.

Knowing that what he was about to say would come as a shock to Randy, but that Randy wouldn't show it, Earl replied, "Let's get this over with. Marta's body is in the kitchen. Why don't we go inside?"

Randy silently followed Earl around to the back of the house. Earl opened the door and motioned Randy to go in ahead of him, a courtesy he probably wouldn't have observed under ordinary circumstances. Randy stood in the doorway, taking time to survey the room before he stepped in. Marta's body was lying on the floor face up, a pool of blood a couple of feet in diameter stretched outward from beneath her hair. Her arms were flung outward, while her right leg lay across her left. No one had straightened her dress, which revealed her right leg up to her mid-thigh. The knife lay on the floor across the room. A plastic plate and cup had somehow ended up in the far corner of the room to Randy's left, in the shadows next to a decrepit armchair. It seemed to Randy that nothing in the room had been touched after Marta died and that this was Earl's way of saying, "I have nothing to hide." In fact, Earl was not intending to make a statement of any kind. It simply had never occurred to Earl to straighten things up. What had happened, had happened, and what would happen, would happen.

Randy then approached Marta's body and deftly checked for a carotid pulse. Finding none, he looked carefully at the body, starting with the floppy head and broken neck. He lifted the head, and after moving it from side to side, gently laid it down again. He then moved methodically down to the torso, arms, hands, fingernails, abdomen, back, legs, and feet, checking for cuts, bruises, blood stains, torn clothing, urine, feces, and so on. Earl felt as if his own mind was being inspected for evidence of guilt, hate, bitterness, relief, jealousy, infidelity, and every foul motivation known to man.

Randy stood, and after taking a deep breath, turned to Earl and said, "Tell me what happened."

Earl said, "I'm no good at telling things. Marta always said that. I might as well start with where it got to. I never expected anything like this from Marta. It was as if something came over her. She came at me with that knife over there on the floor and I turned to get out of the way, and she cut me in the shoulder here. It wasn't anything deep. I tried to get the knife away from her because Warren was sitting there at the table waiting for breakfast, and Melody was standing beside me. I didn't want them to get hurt. I tried to take the knife from her. She was much stronger than I expected and the blade cut me here on my hand, not too bad. I had to do something to stop this from going any further. I'd seen her in a state before, but nothing like this. I didn't plan out what I was going to do. I guess it was instinct, but I charged her the way I did when I was a lineman going at someone. I guess I hit her pretty hard, harder than I'd expected, and she got knocked backward land- ing head first on the floor. I saw her falling like it was in slow motion, like in the movies. It really was like that. I saw her fall- ing back and I knew it was bad because her head was below the rest of her body, so I knew her head was going to hit first, and I knew that was bad. When she didn't move, I went over to see how she was. She wasn't moving or breathing. She was already dead."

Randy looked at Earl and said, "You have no idea why she was so far gone that she went at you with a knife?"

"No, I can't figure it at all."

Randy pressed him. "No idea at all? There wasn't anything going on between the two of you? When you've been married a lot of years, like you and Marta, you get to know someone pretty well, I mean about what's eating at them. No idea at all?"

"No, I'd tell you if I did."

Randy was silent for a while and looked around the kitchen once again. He then said, "Earl, in a dozen years as a sheriff's deputy, I've heard more stories than I can count about how someone got hurt or ended up dead. Since I wasn't there when these things happened, I can only listen to the story and see if it makes sense to me. There are always one or two things that make a story click into place for me, and when that happens I've got a pretty good idea that what I've been told is the truth. Do you understand?"

"No, I'm not sure I do."

"I got to tell you, Earl, and I'm saying this not as a sheriff's deputy, but as someone who has known you a long time and doesn't want to see you get into a tangle with the law here that I don't think you deserve. What I'm saying is that what you've told me doesn't click into place. I don't think you're lying because I know you and that's not your way, so I'm thinking that you're leaving something out, and that's what makes it sound like you're not telling the truth. That's what worries me, Earl. That you'll tell this story and no one will believe you, and you'll get in so deep you won't be able to get out. We're not talking about knocking over someone's fence with your tractor, we're talking about a dead person here."

"I know we are. And I know you're trying to help me, but I've told you best I can what happened. Every word I said is true."

"Earl, let me see if I've got this right. Marta, out of the blue, grabbed a kitchen knife, came at you, stabbed you in the shoulder and then cut your hand as you tried to take the knife away from her, and then you hit her with a football charge so hard it sent her flying into the air so she did a backward dive and landed so she broke her neck and died instantly, and you don't have the foggiest idea why she was trying to stab you."

Earl knew he was leaving out everything that would be most hurtful to Marta if the whole town were to know. But what happened at home in their family, and what happened in the past, were nobody's business but hers. It had nothing to do with what the law needed to know about how she died.

Randy seemed to have a need to get it right, and what he didn't understand bothered him. "Earl, I have to tell you that my experience as a deputy sheriff points me to one conclusion: there must have been an argument—at the very least—that got Marta so riled that she went at you with a knife. People don't do what Marta did for no reason. Even crazy people have their reasons for doing what they do, otherwise they wouldn't be doing them. And crazy people don't just go off and try to stab someone without anyone having a clue that something was brewing."

Earl looked at Randy as if to say that he'd said all he was going to say.

Randy paused before saying, "Earl, I hate to do this to you, but before I go I should talk with the kids, if that's all right with you. You said they were there in the kitchen when all this happened."

Earl called Warren and Melody who were in the shed behind the house watching the kitchen door through the slats as their father and the sheriff were talking inside for what seemed like hours. They knew the man was the sheriff because of the dark green emblem painted on the sides of his car. When their father called for them they delayed coming out for a little bit so as to hide the fact that they'd been spying.

Randy said to them that he was sorry about what happened to their mother and that he knew that this must be very hard on them, but he would like to talk to them, just for a few minutes, to see if they could tell him what happened because everyone sees things that no one else notices.

Randy turned to Melody because she was older and asked her to tell him what happened. She told him the story as her father had told her to tell it, but she told it in a sing-song way that sounded as if she were reciting multiplication tables.

Trying to rephrase his question to get her to stray from the script that Earl had written, Randy asked her if there had been anything she knew of that was churning her mother up lately. Melody couldn't stop herself from saying what she knew because there was finally someone who wanted to hear it. She told the deputy sheriff about the way her mother had been hard on Warren for a long time for no good reason at all. She hesitated before saying the next part because she didn't want to embarrass Warren, but there was no holding back what she had been wanting to say for so long—that her mother had been shamed by Warren's sucking his thumb at his age, and doing it in school where everyone could see, and that she had tried punishing him and that didn't work, and had tried the bad tasting ointment and that hadn't worked either, and finally tried the leather gloves.

Up to this point, Randy had simply listened to Melody and had not interrupted her because she was telling the story very clearly, but he stopped her when she mentioned the leather gloves.

"What kind of gloves are you talking about?"

"Leather gloves that men wear for doing heavy work like chopping wood or loading hay onto trucks. She kept them in the lowest drawer of the kitchen dresser."

"And you say that Warren had to wear them at night?"

"Yes, she put them on Warren at night, and she wrapped leather rope around the wrists so he couldn't take them off—he wouldn't have taken them off because he does what he's told—but she tied them on him to make sure he couldn't get them off."

Randy, trying not to show any feeling about what he was hearing, asked, "For how long did your mother tie the leather gloves on Warren?"

"Only a few days, but I couldn't stand to see it even once, so I untied the gloves after she went to sleep at night and put them back on him early in the morning. That's what pushed her over the edge. She went crazy this morning when she saw that someone had taken the gloves off of Warren. It was me who did it. What I did ended up getting her killed. But I couldn't stand to watch it."

Randy, no longer sounding like a deputy sheriff, said, "Melody, you didn't get her killed. Grown-ups get themselves into trouble and get themselves killed without any help from their children. You were just being a big sister to your brother, a big sister I'd be proud to have."

Tears rolled down Melody's cheeks. She couldn't remember the last time she'd cried, but she knew it had been years. It must have been because her mother had done something very mean to her or Warren, but she couldn't remember what it was because it happened so long ago. Melody felt that when she cried, it made her mother win twice, so she promised herself a long time ago that she would never cry again. She hadn't imagined that it would not be pain, but kindness, that would make her break her vow.

Randy asked Melody to go on telling him what happened. She wiped her nose with her forearm and inhaled deeply. Warren was staring intently at Melody waiting to hear what else she would say. "This morning Daddy and Warren and I came into the kitchen after we finished the chores. She was the worst I've ever seen her. She took one look at us and ordered Warren to show her his right hand. She saw that he'd been sucking his thumb. I don't know how she was so sure, but she was. The gloves hadn't stopped him so she figured Daddy or me had taken them off him and we were ganging up on her. I forget what she said, maybe she didn't say anything, but she grabbed a knife from the top of the dresser next to the stove where the knives and pots are kept and she ran over to where Warren was sitting at the table, and before anyone knew what she was going to do, she grabbed his hand and pushed it down hard on the table. We all knew then that she was going to stab his hand or cut it off or something. That's when Daddy jumped between her and Warren and grabbed her hand that was holding the knife, but she twisted free and she was going after Warren again, and Daddy rammed her and she fell down hard on the floor and she wasn't breathing, and she was dead."

Melody knew that she had not told the sheriff what she had said to her father in the barn—that anyone could see that her mother was crazy and that her father should stop her from treating Warren so horribly. But she figured that keeping that to herself didn't change the fact that her father hadn't done anything wrong: her mother had tried to stab Warren and her father had only tried to stop her. Earl didn't mind that Melody had told the story as she did, even though it made it apparent that he was lying to Randy. It was only right that Melody should tell it that way, he thought, even if he hadn't said it that way himself.

THREE

After listening to Melody's account of what happened that morning, Randy said that he would like to take a few minutes to think about what he had heard and seen before deciding what to do about it. He walked around to the back of the house and went into the kitchen again. The room itself had a strange feel to him, aside from the fact that Marta's dead body was laying on the floor. He had been in hundreds of houses in the course of the past twelve years as a deputy, and this one was different. The whole first floor was a single room, with a bathroom tucked under the stairs to the second floor. The first floors of other houses no bigger than Earl's, were divided into a kitchen, a living room, and sometimes a small dining area next to the kitchen. The undivided first floor of Earl's house gave Randy the feeling that whoever built the house had given up on it, left it unfinished. It looked more like an empty doll's house than a place where a family of four people lived.

From where Randy was standing at the back door of the house, he noticed that all four walls of the room were bare: there wasn't a single family picture, photograph, or children's drawing, not even a calendar or a clock to break up the bleakness of the pale yellow walls that were streaked with grease-laden dust. The rectangular oak table stood stolidly in the middle of the room. Three of the wooden chairs were tucked neatly in place, while the fourth, with its back to him, was pulled out from the table. On the side of the room to Randy's left, a flight of stairs climbed steeply to the second floor with a handrail secured to the wall, but without a banister. The two walls in front and in back of Randy each had two curtainless windows on either side of a door between them. In the far left corner, peering out of the dark, was an easy chair with a small table and lamp next to it. These pieces of furniture seemed unanchored, bearing no connection with anything else in the room.

Marta's body lay a full fifteen feet from the pulled-out chair that must have been Warren's. Blood from Marta's ear had coagulated on the floor. When she was alive, Marta had had a formidable presence, even though she was a small woman, just over five foot tall and not a hundred pounds, Randy reckoned. Earl had driven his large-framed body, which must weigh at least two hundred pounds, shoulder first, into the pocket between her chin and neck. Of course, there is the instinct of a father to protect his children—maybe that's all there was to it—but why had gentle Earl hit Marta so hard that her body was thrown fifteen feet before landing on the back of her head? Why hadn't he simply wrapped his arms tightly around that slight woman? It was true that she had a knife and had cut him twice, and was crazed, but still …

There was no doubt in Randy's mind that Melody's story was more accurate than Earl's. Marta, for reasons that were still a mystery to Randy, seemed to have been extremely cruel to Warren, and had become possessed by the boy's thumb sucking, which embarrassed her—but could that have been enough, even for a madwoman, to go after her own child with a knife, apparently trying to strike the blade through his hand or to cut off his thumb? The measures she took to prevent him from sucking his thumb—ending up with her tying leather gloves on his hands—were undoubtedly extreme. But why had Earl said that she was going after him and not the boy, and why had he left out of his story Marta's use of the ointment and the gloves to break the boy's habit? He had evidently instructed Melody not to mention any of that. The girl's account was a story of believable people doing things for reasons that make sense, even if it's a crazy sense. Earl's story made no sense. He's lying. Who's he protecting—Marta, even after she's dead? Himself? Or is Earl right—she just went mad out of the blue? It's possible that Earl had been blind to Marta's madness. People don't want to admit that a member of the family is going crazy or maybe has already gotten there.

As if waking from a sleep, Randy realized that he was standing not twenty feet from a corpse, which for some reason was not distressing to him. The body was dead and the life of the family was a secret tightly held by the three who survived. From the way Warren huddled behind Melody whenever he had the chance, disconnected from everyone except his sister, Randy sensed that Melody and Warren had created a family of their own from which he and everybody else, including Earl, were barred. Warren had not spoken a single word, and Randy had not pressed him—he was an eleven-year-old whose mother had tied gloves on his hands, and later tried to stab him, or do something worse. He was in shock and had plenty of reason not to want to talk to grown-ups, who as a group had not done particularly well by him.

As Randy walked out of the kitchen, the sun was blinding and the hot, moist air made walking feel like wading through warm water. He stood silently for a moment, removed his hat to wipe the sweat from his brow that had formed during the half hour he had spent in the house. He then turned toward Earl, who was carrying on his shoulder a bag of feed, and said, "Earl, you got a minute?" in a tone that sounded more irritated than he had intended.

"Sure, what do you reckon has to be done?" Earl was aware he was not using Randy's first name because Randy was no longer just a man he had known most of his life, he was the deputy sheriff.

"I wish I could say that just the routine things have to be checked off the list, but I have to ask you again what happened."

"I don't know what I can add to what I already said. Marta came at me with a knife and I had to take it from her as best I could."

"Talking to you is mighty frustrating, you know that, Earl? After Melody gave her version of what happened—a version that sounded much more plausible than yours—I thought for sure that you'd admit that Marta tried to stab the boy, not you. But now you seem to be sticking with your story."

"I keep telling you, Randy, that's the way I saw it. It looked different to Melody, I can't help that."

"Either way—yours or Melody's—I still don't understand how it came to a knife attack on you or the boy. Melody's got her story about Marta going crazy about the boy's thumb sucking and how she completely unraveled when the gloves didn't work. You never mentioned any of that. Are you saying that Marta had not become fierce in her battle with the boy about his thumb sucking? No, let me put it differently because we're at a different stage of things now. Will you say for the record that Melody's story about the thumb sucking and the gloves is what was going on before this attack occurred?"

Earl seemed surprised that Randy had hit him point blank with this question, and what's more, used the words "for the record." He stuttered, "Well ... that's hard to ... I don't know if I could say exactly ... It's just that ... you see ..."

"No, Earl, I don't see. That's the problem. That's been the problem from the beginning. Let me make it simple: is it true that Marta was beside herself about Warren's thumb sucking and that she tried punishing him, putting ointment on his thumbs, lacing leather work gloves on him, and even with all

32

of that she couldn't get him to stop doing it at home and in school and everywhere else?"

Earl, more settled now, said, "I can't say that for the record, no, I can't."

"You do know that if that's the case, all we have is the word of a fifteen-year-old girl which you, her father, can't or won't corroborate. And without a reason for Marta's going over the edge, your story feels thin and it's hard to believe that it's the whole story. And then people have to fill in the rest of the story with things they make up themselves."

"Like what? She came after me and I had to try to keep the children from getting hurt by accident? I can't see anything wrong with what I did."

"Earl, you asked me what reasons people would make up to fill in the holes in your story. There are plenty of reasons she could have gone after you. You could have some woman on the side, or you could have been beating her and the children, or maybe involved in illegal activities, or doing unnatural things that were driving her to distraction."

"You know none of that's true. You know me."

"Earl, to tell you the truth, I don't know for a fact that none of that's true. How could I know? All I have to go on is what I see and what you and the children tell me, and all that's not fitting together, so somebody's twisting the truth, and they must have a good reason for doing it."

On his way back to town, Randy radioed in some of what he had learned, and alerted his boss, the county sheriff, Virgil Ryder, that there was a death at the Bromfman farm that had loose ends to tie up.

After Randy left, Earl told Melody and Warren that their mother's body was still in the kitchen awaiting a coroner's examination that afternoon, and would then be taken by van to the county morgue.

Melody asked her father, "What's a coroner?"

"A doctor who works for the Sheriff's Office. He examines bodies of dead people to see what they died of."

"Doesn't everybody know what she died of? Don't they believe what we told them?"

"They have to make sure."

"Are they saying that you killed her on purpose?"

"No, no one's saying that. The deputy said that people might make up stories about what happened so they have to get all the facts straight with science."

"I don't see what science can tell them that we can't."

"They think science is the truth—not what anybody tells them."

"Are you afraid they'll say you killed her on purpose?" Melody asked.

"No. I know what happened, and you know what happened, and the scientific information can't say something that didn't happen."

"I don't want them making up lies about you. I told the sheriff what happened. Why did you say she was coming after you and not Warren? You know she was going after Warren."

"It doesn't matter whether she was trying to stab Warren or me. I had to stop her either way, and I would have done the same thing either way, so I didn't want the last thing anyone knows about your mother to be that she tried to stab her eleven-year-old boy, something they'll make up ugly gossip about. Let them make up gossip about me, about what I did to get her so mad. Your mother suffered a lot in her life, so why make her suffer more after her death?"

"Do you think she can feel what's happening now?"

"I don't know really. Maybe she can, maybe she can't. But I know I can feel it for her, and I don't want people going around gossiping about her and making up things about you and Warren. She's not the person they would try to make her out to be in their gossip. She had a hard life. Lots of people didn't treat her like she deserved, and I don't want that to continue after she's dead. I know you can understand that."

Melody bored her eyes into her father's. She said, "I guess, but you always defended her, even when she was wrong. It scares me when you lie. You can understand *that*, can't you?"

Earl's eyelids drooped over his bloodhound eyes as he looked at his daughter.

Melody did not relent: "It's too late to say all that you should have said when she was alive. Can't you at least say it now, now that she's dead?"

Earl felt that he had blundered his way through life, and that Melody was pointing out what he had always known but hoped no one would notice—that he was weak.

The only time that Earl was free of the weight of the past and its repercussions in the present was while looking through the dusty window of the combine, taking comfort in the rhythm of the movement of the grain truck moving just ahead of him and to the right, as other people find peace while walking their well-loved dog who assuredly leads the way, occasionally dipping his nose to smell the ground. When driving the combine, which his father had bought when Earl was a boy of fourteen, Earl could feel as his own the power of the large, rock-hard, deeply treaded tires of the machine gripping the soil, never slipping or faltering even on a muddy grade in the rain. Earl had learned that there were skills in wheat farming that could be learned and depended upon, as well as instincts and the capacity for good judgment that could be developed with experience and age—none of which he could say about the way he lived the other parts of his life.

Mercifully for Earl, it was the heart of harvest season, so once Randy finally left, Earl found a hired hand to take the wheel of the grain truck while he climbed the two metal steps to the door of the combine. He had sat next to his father in the old combine during harvest from the time he was four. Earl knew the sounds, smells, and vibrations of the machine like he knew the feel of his heart beating in his chest. Over the background growl of the engine he could hear the hiss of the cutting bar as it slashed the wheat stalks at their base, hurling them into the huge rotating threshing drum. While driving the combine, Earl's gaze was fixed on the row of wheat stalks directly ahead of him, but out of the corner of his eye he saw at one o'clock the orange-yellow cloud of powdered grain floating like a halo over the deep bed of the grain truck as it lumbered down the field.

After the supper dishes were put away, Warren and Melody went to their room on the upper floor as they always did, but this time was different. They weren't going there to get away from their mother, they were going there to talk about her no longer being there. Once the door was shut, they each got onto their own bed. They sat up facing the wall opposite the head of their beds, which were placed next to one another with a small rectangular table between the two. This was the position they always took when talking to one another in their room. The square room, with its peeling wallpaper, had a closet (in which Melody and Warren changed their clothes in private), and a makeshift dresser that Earl had made from crates in which machinery is shipped. The sole window, above the table, looked out onto the rear farmyard.

"Are you glad she's dead?" Warren asked.

"She was the worst person I've ever known. I don't know any other mothers, except in books, but I think she was the worst mother I've ever heard of." Melody was a reader who took out two books at a time from the town library, not caring what they were about, and returning them for two new ones within a few days.

"She wasn't doing mean things all the time," Warren said, checking to see if it was all right to be glad your mother is dead even if you were willing to admit that she wasn't bad every second of every day.

"Aren't you glad she's dead?" Melody asked.

"Yeah, but I keep thinking she's still alive. Can dead people do anything to you?"

"No, 'course not."

"Do you think she can hear us now?" Warren asked. He didn't know much of anything about what happens after you're dead and was relieved that Melody wasn't making him feel stupid for it.

"No, I told you, she's gone, there's nothing left of her except her dead body, and they're going to bury that."

"Miss Wells said that when we die we go to a place where we meet everyone we've ever loved and who've loved us," Warren said.

"Even if that were true, she didn't love us, so we wouldn't meet her there. If there's a hell, that's where she is right now." They both laughed, which helped to release the tension in their bodies as they said these things that they knew no one should say even if they were true.

"I can't really believe she's gone," Warren said.

"It was strange having supper without anyone sitting in her chair even though I was glad she wasn't in it," Melody said. "I used to watch her out of the corner of my eye to try to be ready for whatever she might do. She almost always did something worse than I expected, like smack my knuckles hard with a fork if I reached for something."

"Do you think Daddy's glad she's dead?" This was the second biggest question Warren had, next to whether Melody was glad she was dead.

"I don't know what goes on in Daddy's head. I think he's glad, but not all glad."

"What do you mean, 'not all glad'"?

"I don't know why he ever married her. He's a nice person and she isn't … I mean wasn't," Melody said.

"She was mean to him too, so how could he be 'not all glad' she's dead?"

"I don't know. I never knew why he stood up for her even when he knew what she did was wrong. Not just wrong, horrible. I guess that's what you're supposed to do if you're married. That's why I'm never going to get married."

Warren finally felt free to say what he had been wanting to say. "I think he's stupid. If he liked her, he can't be very smart. If he married her, he's got to be an idiot. 'Cause he stood up for things she did that he knew were horrible, then he's a coward too."

Warren scared himself as he said these things out loud, but he went on. "We didn't have a mother who wanted us. Once in a while, when he wasn't standing up for her, I liked him, but that never lasted very long."

Warren couldn't allow himself to continue this line of thought because it was leading to the conclusion that he was now an orphan.

"I wonder if he'll get married again," Melody said.

"I doubt it. I think he's learned his lesson."

"But he likes being in a family. You can see how much he loves Grampa, and Gramma before she died, and still loves Uncle Paul and Aunt Leslie. Gramma and Aunt Leslie made real families—everyone in the family likes the others—at least most of the time—and they look out for one another. I'm sure Daddy wanted a family like that, but that was impossible with her as his wife."

"Do you think he loves us?" Warren asked, getting to still another question that was burning in him. "He never does anything with us except farm work and takes us with him to town in the truck when he has something to do there, and he hardly ever says anything to us."

Melody liked talking with Warren. He was thinking all the time and noticed things she didn't. Warren not only saw things she hadn't, he could say them, which is very unusual for a boy his age—actually for a boy or man of any age, she thought. Melody thought Warren was smarter than she was, but that no one else knew it because he said almost nothing to anybody but her. Melody was a pretty girl whose brown hair seemed to frame her face, which in turn framed her beautiful green eyes. She was tall, more than half a foot taller than her mother, and looked older than her age. Strangers sometimes mistook her for her mother's younger sister. Warren thought she was the prettiest girl in the school. He wished she could be his girlfriend, but he knew that wasn't allowed, so he'd have to settle for her being his sister.

Warren and Melody had an unspoken agreement not to talk about anything related to sex. Of course, Warren was well aware that Melody was now wearing a bra—a word he'd heard other boys use at school—and that for years she had been doing something in the bathroom with boxes of things that he didn't understand, but he knew it had to do with girls and women. He had begun to have wet dreams, which scared him, but he would never tell Melody about that.

"It feels like everything's changed," Melody said. "The house has changed, Daddy's changed, the farm has changed. I'm the same, but everything else is different, except you, you're the same too."

Warren didn't think that everything was different. In fact, he didn't think *anything* was different, and that was what worried him. Warren could feel *her* presence in the house and in their father, and worst of all, in himself. He thought that it would be too frightening for Melody if he were to say this out loud, so he kept it to himself.

"What would happen if Daddy died? Would they let us live here on our own?" Warren asked. "It would be fine with me if they did."

"They'd never let a fifteen-year-old and an eleven-year-old do that. How would we earn enough money to take care of ourselves?"

"We could sell the farm and live in this house if they let us stay. We could tell whoever bought it that that was a condition of the deal."

"There are laws. You have to be sixteen or eighteen, I forget which, to live on your own."

"How would they know? They might think that the person who bought the farm was taking care of us. You know that we don't really need anyone to take care of us. We don't need to be told when to have breakfast or how to make our beds or that we should go to school."

"I don't think they understand that. They think we're still babies."

"After we sell the farm, we could move somewhere else, and say that you're sixteen and that you're looking after me. You look older than sixteen and you know it."

"Warren, why are you going on like this? Daddy's alive and he's not sick or old or anything, so we can just live here and do what we've been doing."

"But you don't know what's going to happen."

"What on earth are you talking about, Warren?"

"This morning, she was alive and at the same time she was just about to die, but she didn't know it, or she knew it and she didn't care, or couldn't do anything about it. The same is true for Daddy. He's alive today, but we're in the middle of something that's gotten her killed, and it could just as easily get him killed. It's not over."

Melody didn't brush Warren off this time. Warren was right that something had broken loose in the house and already one person was dead, and it was possible that their father would die. He wasn't good at taking care of himself—look who he married. And there were ways in which he was a coward, which could get a person killed. But when she went after Warren with a knife, he stopped her in the strongest way anyone could have: he smashed her and killed her. So why, Melody wondered, had he told her not to mention anything about the way her mother hated Warren and how she tried to prevent him from sucking his thumb, and how she had put the gloves on his hands, and

40

especially not to say anything about her trying to stab his hand with a knife?

That night Warren woke up screaming, which awakened Melody with a start. He said, "I dreamt that Earl was twisting her head until it came off and I could hear the bones snapping in her neck like it sounds when you step on dry branches. I don't know if I heard her bones break when Earl rammed her in the neck or if it was only in the dream."

Both Melody and Warren were surprised that Warren was calling their father Earl, but neither of them said anything about it. From that point on, Warren used their father's first name when he was talking with Melody, but never with anyone else.

Randy Larsen showed up at the farm in the late afternoon of the day following Marta's death. He came when he did because he didn't want to take Earl away from the harvesting. In fact, Earl had been in something of a daze and had lost control of the systematic way he had harvested his fields for the previous fifteen years. Several of the wheat farmers whose fields were near Earl's could see from the sporadic appearance of his combine that Earl would not be able to complete the harvest on his own. Without a word said to Earl about the matter, the neighboring farmers took turns using their own equipment and hired hands to work Earl's fields for him.

When Randy got out of his car, he again told Earl how sorry he was that his family was going through such troubled times, and he seemed to mean it. As was his way, he apologized to Earl for intruding on him at a time like this, but it had to be done. He said that Sheriff Ryder had asked him to search the house, but he would need a search warrant unless Earl said it was okay. Earl told Randy to go right ahead, he had nothing to hide, and he would help Randy locate things he might be interested in. Randy thanked him and said that he would be out the next day with a couple of other deputies to help him. There would be no reason for Earl to interrupt his harvesting work unless he wanted to be there during the search. When

Earl got home the next evening the search had been completed and Randy had left a note thanking Earl for his cooperation.

It was all so polite you'd never know it was a murder investigation, Warren thought. Melody took comfort in the deputy sheriff's low-key approach. Warren knew that something wasn't right about his mother's death. He'd been almost as close to his mother's neck as his father was when Earl drove his shoulder into his mother's neck. Warren was convinced now that the bones he had heard snapping in his dream weren't sounds he'd made up, they were the sounds he'd heard as his mother's neck was breaking, and those sounds were now permanently in his head.

FOUR

Once the children were bedded down, Earl sat by himself on the front porch of the house. He did something he had loved to do when he was a boy, and had loved to do with Warren and Melody when they were small. He held his hand a half-foot in front of his face. With all the lights out in the house, the darkness was complete: he couldn't see even the dimmest outline of his hand. Earl found the absolute absence of light both wondrous and frightening. The throbbing din of crickets filled the void left by blindness. With his feet up on the railing, Earl sat tilted back on one of the metal kitchen chairs. When he lit a cigarette, he could see for a flickering instant the other three chairs gathered round him like children waiting to be told a story. The chairs, each with a torn red vinyl seat, had been left in a heap of odds and ends by a neighbor after selling his farm and loading in the back of his truck all that he felt was worth salvaging from his twenty-five thankless years of wheat farming. It was hard for Earl to believe that he had killed Marta earlier that same day.

Earl was alone for the first time since he awoke that morning before dawn. He recalled his mother's words when he told her that he and Marta had gotten married at the county seat: "What promise there is for the two of you." Of all the words she could have used, she used the word "promise." During his years with Marta there had been promises that had been made and broken, promises that had never been made, promises he had made to her that might still be kept, promises neither of them had thought to make because they had no idea that people made such promises to one another. For Earl, youth itself had been a promise of good things to come, but in looking back on his hopes, he found them spectacularly naïve.

He, in his full-throated innocence, happened upon Marta in January of their sophomore year at the northern campus of the state university. On first catching sight of her on the main quad, he thought Marta was extraordinarily beautiful. She did not carry herself with the sway and swagger of girls who felt the power of their beauty. As a varsity football player in high school, Earl had been desirable to the cheerleader set, which he enjoyed, but he never overcame his feelings of awkwardness around girls. Girls had always seemed to Earl to be better than boys at the game that high school kids played. It was as if girls were born knowing the strategies, and like confident, experienced chess players, instinctively knew what moves to make. On top of that, the game was rigged by the colossal advantage held by girls, whose newly created breasts had the power to reduce boys to gawking idiots.

To his surprise, Earl, who had been a middling student in high school, had done well academically during his first three semesters at the university. Even more unexpected, he had found the courses—particularly English, philosophy, and mathematics—genuinely absorbing. Earl was thrilled by the fact that the university was overflowing with people he had never met. During the first eighteen years of his life there had been about sixty children close to his age with whom he grew up. They had become so familiar to him that he could predict with almost perfect accuracy what each of them was going to say to him when they crossed paths. Since leaving home, he had not for a moment felt homesick.

Though he continued to feel awkward around girls and their breasts at the university, Earl became increasingly free to take his chances with girls for two reasons: first, he recognized that he was more intelligent than he had ever supposed and that some girls liked that, and second, he developed the conviction that he had nothing to lose in taking his chances with girls. The logic of the latter belief was fairly simple—he did not have a girlfriend, he wanted to have a girlfriend, and while being turned down by a girl would be disappointing, it would not be devastating because there were other things in his life now, the most important of which was the pride he took in the ways he could use his mind. In addition, he had developed relationships with "guys" his age that were of a quality and intensity that he had never before experienced with anyone. Earl was painfully aware that his use of the term "guys" to refer to his male friends, and himself, was an evasion of a problem. He had all the physical characteristics of a man, but that alone did not make him a man. His father was a man, his older brother was a man, but Earl did not feel he had earned the right to call himself a man. And yet, he felt that the word "boy" did not fit him either. And "young man" was the name his fifth grade teacher used to address him when he had been caught firing a spitball at someone across the aisle.

It was in this state of mind that Earl first laid eyes on Marta. She was a striking figure. Her black hair, which had the sheen of the feathers of a raven, was cut in bangs that crisply traversed her forehead before falling straight down to her neck where it turned a sharp right angle to travel around the sides and back of her head. Her black hair drew a razor sharp line as it crossed the pale skin of her cheeks and forehead, a pallor so starkly white that it seemed to be forcefully resisting any shades of red or brown that might attempt to give color from within. Why Earl was attracted by such a forbidding figure he would never know, but drawn to her he was. He at first tried to insinuate himself into her life by waiting for her to show up at the campus cafeteria and then take a seat at the table she chose. She was always with a group of other students who seated themselves around a large table. This black-haired girl seemed not to notice him, rarely looked in his direction, and seemed somehow effortlessly to direct the flow of conversation away from him.

But Earl persisted. Eventually, he happened upon her when she was standing in the lobby of the library talking with another girl. He brazenly walked up to them and said, "Mind if I join you?" Marta, who was even prettier close up than she was at a distance, looked blankly at him in a way that was more dismissive than her telling him outright to get lost. He had never experienced anything like this. Rather than feeling deflated, he found the situation humorous. In fact, he felt invulnerable—he now believed that he had absolutely nothing to lose because she was showing herself to be a type of girl he did not particularly like.

Having made himself impossible to ignore, he was able to engage Marta and her friend in a brief conversation, although Marta seemed to be trying to find an excuse to rush off somewhere. She was a bristly girl who did not talk much, quite unlike the high school cheerleaders who could not stop talking.

Earl, staring into the night, thought about who the people he and Marta were when they first met. He felt a deep sorrow well up in him. He had been attracted to her, he now thought, because she was unreachable. He wondered if he had ever been as taken by who she was as by who she was not. He had never known a person so bereft as she. Had he romanticized her suffering or had he simply ignored it in his pursuit of a pretty girl? Or was it something else? She was unapproachable, unknowable. As distinctive to Earl as his fingerprints was the fact that from the time he was thirteen or fourteen, probably earlier, he felt an unquenchable desire to know, as he assumed everyone did, what it was like for other people to live their lives, and how living their life was different from or the same as what it was like for him to live his, and what differences there were between life in his family and life in the families of other people, and what it was like to be a girl or a Jew or an old man, and to know innumerable other things about what it was like to live a life other than his own. By knowing about others' lives, he was certain that he would know more about what it was to live his own. He felt that to know in this way was not a philosophical hobby, but the foundation on which to build his life.

Earl couldn't believe that everyone his age was not burning to know the answers to these sorts of questions. He felt a great sense of urgency about finding answers to his questions because it seemed to him, on the basis of what he saw in the people in his family and in his friends' families and in school, that once you turned twenty, something died in you, and you lost interest in these sorts of questions. It seemed that when you became responsible for your own life and the life of your wife and children, an insurmountable wall grew in you that separated you from the need to respond to these questions. This type of questioning was "useless" in that it had nothing to do with your ability to provide for yourself and your family or to advance your career.

These questions, he was convinced, were a luxury of childhood, like the free room and board children are given, and the long summer vacations during which they are free to do anything they want. He reasoned that, just as the loss of free room and board and long summer vacations was not felt as a great sacrifice because it was more than balanced by the freedom that became yours as an adult, so too, the loss of the awareness of these questions and the need to answer them were more than offset by the pride of "know-how," which was the distinctive mark of maturity, the key to liberation from childhood awkwardness and self-consciousness. Adult know-how brought with it a calm self-possession that you can see in the hands of a man fixing a machine or hear in the sure, strong sound of the voice of the school principal speaking on the public address system. What adults know, they know with surety—they are certain of it in a way that a child never is. Earl reckoned that becoming self-possessed in this way is so irresistible that the need to answer questions of the sort that were important to him doesn't have the chance of a snowball in hell when one has to choose between the two.

Even though he thought everyone under twenty was consumed, as he was, by the wish to talk about their questions, Earl never dared ask his friends, his brother, or his sister any of his questions. He worried that his need to ask the questions—particularly the ones about what it felt like to be a girl—meant that he was a homosexual. He was not sure what a homosexual was because he had never met one, and no one he knew had either, but for some reason he thought that pondering in the way that he did was excessively inward and therefore effeminate. He knew he was excited by girls and not by boys, although, if he was honest with himself, as he sometimes could be, he did once in a while think about a boy. Earl had hoped that he would make friends in college who might talk with him about these things before it was too late, before he forgot his questions in the way that he was amnesic to almost everything that had happened in his life before he was three or four.

From this perspective, it seemed strange to Earl that he had been drawn to Marta, for whom it was apparent from the outset that talking about his questions, or hers, if she still had any, was anathema to her. There were plenty of other pretty girls with whom he could have tried his luck who might have been more interested in thinking and talking in the way that he did. But on that bracing January day when he first laid eyes on Marta, his mind was not focused on finding someone with whom he could talk about his questions. He was more interested in finding a pretty girl to make out with, and maybe to do even more, although the "even more" was beyond him at the time.

Earl's persistence with Marta paid off, although he was not sure why. She had agreed at first to go to evening lectures given by visiting politicians, poets, and scientists. The names of these speakers—Frost, Auden, Stevenson, Rusk, Pauling, Salk—and a good many of the poems that the poets read, and the speeches the others gave, were still vivid in Earl's mind all those years later as he sat on the porch the night Marta died.

He and Marta talked and drank coffee after the lectures, but coffee was not followed by sex. They said goodnight and went back to their dorm rooms. Earl was growing to like Marta in a way he had never before liked anyone. It was not simply that she was pretty, he found her unapologetic strangeness enticing. She did not seem to aspire to being like everyone else, nor did she try to convince anyone she was different. She did not seem to care what anyone thought of her. Marta steadfastly refused to talk about herself. She was very vague about where she grew up, what her parents did, how many brothers and sisters she had, and was closed to questions having to do with her childhood, such as whether she had a best friend, how she got along with her parents and her brothers and sisters (if she had any), how she liked school, and so on. Earl very soon stopped asking her almost anything about her life—past or present. The fact that they began to make out after a few weeks was enough for Earl at the time.

Marta liked Earl or she would have dropped him very early on. She liked his looks even though he was not classically handsome—his face was a little too square, his ears too big, and the cleft in his chin too deep. That he was a tall, broad-shouldered man who was comfortable in his large-framed body appealed greatly to Marta. As pretty as Marta was, she had never had a boyfriend. The whole idea of it—as she saw her friends going about it—seemed to be the opposite of what she wanted. Why would she sign up for another round of being the possession of a man, which every girl she knew thirsted for—they wanted to "give themselves" to a guy. The idea of belonging to a guy or anyone else was repugnant to Marta.

Marta's abhorrence of the idea of being "pinned" to a guy was evident to Earl from the outset, but that did not bother him because he wasn't in love with her and had no desire to be "pinned" to her. He liked her complete rejection of the usual script for college romances. They spent a lot of time together and began to feel a bit more at ease with one another, but things were never easy with Marta. One evening they were watching a television newscast in the basement of one of the few dormitories that had a TV. There was coverage of a protest march outside the gates of a state penitentiary where a man was going to be executed in the electric chair. People were chanting, "Stop the killing" and placards read, "One murder doesn't justify another" and "What would Jesus say?" Marta, very upset by what she was seeing, said, "What about the parents of the eight-year-old boy he killed? Isn't it only right that they get justice? That man killed their son and he should pay for it with his life."

Earl knew Marta well enough not to argue the point with her. He did not have strong feelings about capital punishment and could see the validity of both sides of the argument. Trying not to make trouble with Marta, he said, "A person should know that if he kills, he's putting his own life on the line too."

Marta screamed at him, her voice trembling, "Be a man for God's sake. Say what you think, not what you think I want you to say. If you're only a yes-man, I might as well be talking to myself."

Earl was shaken by Marta's tirade. She stared at him waiting for a response like a boxer impatiently bouncing on his toes waiting for his opponent to get up from the mat. Earl finally said, "How can I think anything while you're yelling at me?"

Marta turned away in disgust.

Earl said, "You don't want to talk, you want to fight. You're angry at the world and I'm the only one around to take it out on, and I'm beginning to get sick of it."

That summer between their sophomore and junior years, Earl and Marta moved into an inexpensive attic apartment just across the street from the northwest edge of the campus. Neither of them raised the question of the symbolic significance of their decision to live together. They treated it as a practical matter—neither of them liked dorm life, and the apartment cost each of them less than what they'd been paying for a room in the dorms. Marta insisted that they rent a two-bedroom apartment so she could have a place of her own to study. They would sleep in the same bed in one or the other's bedroom, but they would each have their own room. That was all right with Earl. The alcoholic landlady who lived on the ground floor of this four-storey house didn't care if Earl and Marta were married. All that mattered was that they pay the rent on the first of the month.

By this point, Earl's need to talk about his questions was regaining some of the intensity that it had had before he met Marta. He began to worry that he would lose interest in his questions and that he probably wouldn't notice their disappearance even as it was happening. Earl was well aware that if anything was going to happen on that front with Marta, he would have to take the lead, and Marta would either follow or she wouldn't. The sex they were having once a week wasn't as exciting as he'd expected. Marta showed little interest in sex, and there too, Earl recognized that if anything was going to change, he was the one who would have to try to change it.

Earl was more interested in changing the way they talked than in changing the way they had sex. He made his first attempt on a hot July afternoon when he and Marta were lying on their backs next to one another while a rotating portable fan tenuously balanced on a chest of drawers cooled them with intermittent waves of air.

He began by saying, "I've always wondered about things that other people don't seem to wonder about." As he started, Earl felt Marta tighten up, anticipating some terrible revelation

51

about masturbation or something else she did not want to know about.

But he continued, "It seems strange to me that now, at nineteen, I feel that the best part of my life is over—the best part was the years from the time I was six or seven until I was about ten or eleven. There's nothing better in life than to ride your bicycle over to a friend's house and take a BB gun and shoot bottles or burn tent caterpillar nests, or chase cats, or throw stones through the hole of an old tire, or walk along the railroad tracks putting your ear to the rail to see if a train was anywhere near, or make up a game and work out the rules until everyone agreed on them and then not bother to play the game because something else came along that we couldn't resist, specially in the summer when the days were long. We were boys, and we all liked being boys, we enjoyed things boys like to do."

Earl paused and then said, "You know, I'm sure I'm boring you because I'm boring myself. I'm making up a fairy tale about that part of my life. I wasn't Tom Sawyer or Huckleberry Finn. My family was a farm family and we all had jobs from the time we were five or so. When you grow up on a farm, everyone in the family has a full-time job as a farm worker, and the rest of life is something extra that you squeeze in on the side if you can. You go to school and you have a little free time to do the things I was talking about, but I never had nearly as much of that part of childhood as the kids from town. There wasn't time for me to have friends in the way they did. I never had a best friend. But most of the time I didn't miss that. I'd look forward all year to harvest time in August. Things got wild then. We'd work from the time the sun came up until it set at about 8:00 or 8:30 at night. We—my father, brother, and I, and about a half-dozen hired hands—were like working and eating machines. My mother and sister and some women from town made a huge breakfast before sunrise—a half dozen eggs apiece, bacon, cheese, bread."

Marta smiled, which emboldened Earl.

52

"I'm not exaggerating. Then we'd work like crazy till mid-morning when we had a snack of two or three huge ham sandwiches, milk, cake, and more. When I got to be about four-teen, I got to drive the truck that the combine dumps the wheat kernels into. Every so often, we'd stop and I'd climb into the back of the truck and use a huge shovel to spread out the wheat so it didn't pile up in one part of the bed of the truck and spill over the side. I know I've told you two stories—a lonely farm boy story and a home on the range story. Both stories are true, and they're both lies. Look, I'm going on too long, even for me, so I'll shut up now."

After Earl stopped, Marta was relieved to find that he did not expect her to repay him in kind. He had just wanted her to listen. She had questions and stories of her own, but none like the one he had told. Hers were all about terrifying things that were too painful and embarrassing to remember, much less talk about. And hers were not stories in the sense of having a beginning, middle, and end. What she had were fragments of memories and frozen images. She admired Earl for saying what he had, even though talk like that scared her. And she was deeply grateful to him for not demanding that she do something similar.

Later that summer Earl told Marta that there was some-thing he had wondered about for a very long time. "As a kid I thought my older brother, Paul, was the coolest kid ever born, and he really was. I still feel that way. He was nothing like my friends' older brothers who never included them in things they were doing with their friends. They told the kid brother to get lost, called him a runt, punched him in the arm hard to get rid of him. Even though he was six years older than me, Paul almost always included me, even when he and his friends were playing baseball and I was hardly able to hit a ball because I was, say, seven, when they were, say, thirteen or fourteen. He and his friends played the game in a way that it didn't matter that I wasn't any good compared to them. I was on one of the teams for real, and both teams really wanted to win.

"I don't know how he did it or why he did it, but I felt so good playing with them. I felt loved by him in a way that was different from the way I felt loved by my mother and father. They had to love me, he didn't. And even after he left home, his friends came by to talk to me. They really liked me and didn't look down on me as a tag-along little brother.

"Even after he left home and moved to Indiana, he'd call a lot. If my father answered the phone, which he usually did, Paul would disguise his voice and ask to speak to me, as if he were a friend of mine who my father didn't know, and my father would hand me the phone. Paul knew that if my father knew it was him, he'd want to speak to him, and then my mother would, and he'd be tired of talking by the time I got to talk to him.

"Paul did that for my parents and sister too. When he called, he would call to speak to one of them. He didn't want two of them on the line at the same time or even on the same call. I'll always love him for the way he did that. But when Paul got married, I hardly ever heard from him. I thought he was a fraud, and that he had just been acting like a perfect older brother, and had never really liked me or enjoyed being with me. I was so mad at him and feeling so sorry for myself that I didn't call him either. And then when he did call, I would just sulk and not talk to him about the things we both liked to talk about, like the St. Louis Cardinals who we both loved. I've never talked to him about baseball or much of anything else since he got married. I don't know how other younger brothers feel about their older brothers. I've never asked because I've been afraid of acting like a jilted lover. Even now, talking to you, I feel like a whiner. I didn't do my part in repairing what we had, and I think it's dead now."

As Marta listened to Earl, she didn't sympathize with him much. She would have given anything to have had someone

54

who looked after her the way Paul had looked after Earl, and she did think he was whining. Her mind was elsewhere. She was thinking about a question of her own that she didn't like thinking about. But she thought that if she were ever to tell Earl about any of the questions that she had, there was one that might not be too frightening or embarrassing to tell—but she didn't want to say it then. It was a question that had been with her for as long as she could remember: she didn't know if it was abnormal to hate your own father, not just dislike him, but hate him, to want to kill him, and to hate the whole of your childhood because he was in it.

Earl continued to tell Marta his questions and memories, and Marta, despite herself, came to look forward to hearing them. Earl had grown up in a kind of family that she hadn't believed existed outside of storybooks. Sometimes she didn't believe his stories. The childhood he described was not without its troubles, but they were not big troubles, and they didn't last for years and decades. Earl had grown to hate the life of a wheat farmer, and hated the pressure he felt to take over the farm when he grew up, but he had not grown to hate his father or mother. At first Earl's stories about his family bored her, then they made her angry, which she kept to herself, and then she found them increasingly painful to listen to. She supposed that people would say she was jealous, but she didn't feel jealous. In fact, feeling jealous would have been a relief from not knowing what she was feeling, although she did know it was painful to feel it. Although Earl invited Marta many times to come home with him to meet his parents, she refused to go, and would not tell him why.

One evening when they were lying next to one another in bed after dinner, Marta girded herself to tell Earl a story of her own. She felt terribly self-conscious. "I had a high school principal named Miss Saunders. She liked me, I think, and thought I was smart, but I didn't feel smart at all even though I always got A's. In grammar school some of the teachers felt sorry for how bored I was and sent me to the school administration office to read or do whatever I wanted. The high school was much bigger than the grammar school and middle school because they bussed kids a long way and combined all the kids who had been to four different middle schools. Anyway, Miss Saunders was the principal of the high school and she did the hiring of all the teachers and would come to all the classrooms once in a while and taught whatever the class was studying for part of a class period. So she got to know all the kids. She was a wonderful teacher and the kids and the teachers loved her.

For some reason, she took an interest in me. She told me that what I wrote in my homework papers about books was interesting—not just good for a high school student, but good because the ideas were new to her and made her think. She told me that there was a whole world out there that I couldn't see from inside the walls surrounding the group of small towns in which all the kids in the school lived. I remember her using that expression about the walls around the group of small towns, because it really did feel as if the towns were surrounded by a wall. She said that the door to that world outside of the walls was the state university. It had been years since any student in that high school had gone to college. Miss Saunders helped me get an application form and a form for applying for a scholarship. She didn't have any children of her own. When my parents heard about this—I don't know how they found out—they were ferociously against my going to college. They said I was thinking I was too good for them—who did I think I was? They couldn't prevent me from applying to State, but they refused to fill out the scholarship forms in which they were asked to state their income. Miss Saunders never gave her approval in so many words, but she helped me fill out the application and scholarship forms. I made up an income figure for them that I thought was pretty accurate, and signed my father's name on the application."

Earl listened as she spoke, but didn't interrupt with questions. When she finished, he didn't say anything because he knew she would experience anything he said as patronizing.

Like Marta, Earl had never thought of going to college. Earl knew he didn't want to be a farmer, and in particular, he didn't want to take over the family farm from his father. When he heard that he could probably get a football scholarship that would pay part of the cost of going to State and he could work for the rest, he jumped at it. Year after year, he had seen his father and the other farmers go through the same cycle of fertilizing, planting, growing, and harvesting wheat, and at the end of each year, find themselves exactly where they started. It seemed to him at the time that after the first few years they had learned all there was to learn about wheat farming—they didn't become better farmers, they just became older farmers. The weather, the locusts, and the plant diseases determined how good a harvest you'd get. He and Marta agreed completely on one thing: the worst thing in the world that could happen to them would be to end up farmers like their parents. That deeply held shared conviction comprised a powerful strand of the tie between them. This strand, unfortunately, was only the first of the cruel ironies that bound them irrevocably to one another.

FIVE

I n the days immediately following Marta's death, Earl, Warren, and Melody were surprised by the way in which the rhythms of life on the farm seemed oblivious to Marta's absence. Without uttering a word about what they were doing, they seamlessly took over the various chores that had been Marta's. Her absence did not leave a hole, it opened a space. Earl was aware of how different this was from the weeks and months following the departure of his parents from the farm. They moved East when Melody was six and Warren two. Earl's father, Henry, was no longer able to tolerate the damp, cold Mid-West winters, which caused his arthritis to flare to the point that he could barely walk. They moved to North Carolina, near Earl's sister Leslie and her family. Flora, Earl's mother, died of pancreatic cancer six or seven years after the move.

Earl was surprised by how infrequently he thought of his mother, but in a way it made complete sense. She had been less a discrete character in his life than she had been the stage on which his life was played and the audience for whom the play was performed. What was important was important because it was important to her. With her children she could be finicky about having things done right—not starting to eat before everyone was seated at the table, not slipping into sloppy language such as the use of words like "ain't," double negatives such as "don't want none," and the use of adjectives as adverbs, as in phrases such as "ran pretty good"—but she was rarely morally judgmental. Though Flora had not attended college, she was a very intelligent woman who liked nothing better than to talk with the minister about the sermons he delivered, particularly when her understanding of the piece of scripture from which he had read differed from his. The parables were, for her, commentaries on everyday life lived by ordinary people, not descriptions of the godly behavior of saints and the Savior. Neither did Flora view the minister himself as different from her or anybody else. She didn't hesitate to tell him when she thought a member of the congregation or a family could use a visit from him because of the comfort he could provide in the wake of a sorrow, a disappointment, or an embarrassment. She accepted people for who they were and did not ask them to be anyone else—all three of her children felt this keenly. When Earl, his brother Paul, and Leslie were talking about their mother soon after her death, they were surprised to learn that they each had secretly believed that they were her favorite, and they were all correct in feeling that. Each of them was different and she loved each of them differently, and loved each best.

The contrast between Marta and Earl's mother could not have been greater, and yet Flora warmly welcomed Marta into the family, seeing immediately how profoundly damaged a soul Marta was, and how very hard she worked to keep that to herself. Marta reminded Flora of the injured birds that Earl, as a young boy, had brought home and tried to nurse back to health. He would again and again offer water to the birds with a medicine dropper, but they always turned their beaks away, not knowing he was trying to help them. None of them survived.

These thoughts were running through Earl's mind as he straightened up the first-floor room after dinner, while Warren and Melody were out back talking and throwing stones from a distance into a bucket that they had filled with water from the well. During the two years that Earl and Marta shared the attic apartment near the campus, Marta had mentioned only once that she had a younger sister. She said that she had lost touch with her a few years earlier, and that the last anyone had heard of her she was traveling rough with a man seven or eight years older than she was. Marta had made it clear in her unspoken way that that was all that she was going to say about her sister and that Earl was not to ask any questions, even to ask her name.

Earl recalled vividly the afternoon in the early summer between their junior and senior years at State when he first met Marta's sister. There was a knock on the door of the apartment, which was highly unusual because Earl and Marta lived a sequestered life in their attic. When he opened the door, he immediately knew it was Marta's sister because of the strong family resemblance. She had Marta's oval face, but her hair was a reddish chestnut color and was longer and wavier than Marta's, which gave her a younger, softer look. She was wearing white jeans and a lime green nylon windbreaker over a yellow tee shirt. A blue canvas backpack leaned against her left leg like a beloved dog. They introduced themselves—her name was Anne.

"Is Marta expecting you?"

"No, I'm the kind of person no one expects, and everyone is sorry when I show up."

"How've you managed to establish such a bad reputation in such a short time?"

"Well, it's not that hard. All you have to do is drop out of high school, hang out with unemployed drunks, and have no permanent address."

Earl was taken by the sparkle in the eyes of this very pretty girl.

Anne said, "I'm afraid that Marta is going to have a conniption fit when she comes home and finds me here."

"Is that knapsack all that you have?" Earl asked.

"Yeah, I don't need much—no cocktail dresses or business suits or anything. And I must have lost my make-up kit along the way. Are you the boyfriend? The fiancé? The husband?"

"To tell you the truth I'm not sure what I am. I'm not her fiancé or her husband, that much I'm certain of, but I'm not sure she'd call me her boyfriend."

"Well, we're in the same boat—I'm not sure she'd call me her sister. I don't know if her being my sister means anything more to her than the fact that we happened to grow up in the same house with the same mother and father."

"Does she mean anything more to you than that?" Earl asked.

Anne seemed surprised by this interruption of her banter.

She said, "You know, that's a good question. We were both trying to save our own hides, which was pretty much a full-time job for each of us, so we didn't have much left over to notice if there were other offspring in the house."

Earl had never met anyone quite as quick as this girl.

"Marta left home when she was seventeen," Anne said. "After that, Mom and Daddy—it feels strange calling them by those names—they outnumbered me. Marta lived with the school principal for her last year of high school. So I was alone with them for two years after Marta left. I lived with an aunt and uncle for my last year of high school. I've been on the road for the past year."

"I thought you said you dropped out of high school?"

"I said that for theatrical effect. If we spend any time together, you'll either grow to hate me or you'll get used to that."

"The decision about your staying with us isn't up to me."

62

"What makes you think I want to stay with the two of you?"

"I'm … so … sorry," Earl stuttered. "You're right. You haven't asked for anything. Please come in. What are we doing out on the landing for all this time?" Anne picked up her knapsack and followed Earl a few steps into the apartment.

"I don't want to keep you from what you were doing before I barged in here," she said.

"You didn't barge in. You knocked on the door and I invited you in. Why don't you put your stuff in the study, which is a fancy word for a closet that has bookshelves and a desk in it. It's the last door down the hall on your right. Make yourself at home there or in the living room, which is on your left. Marta should be back in a couple of hours."

Earl met Marta on the landing outside the apartment late in the day when he heard her climbing the stairs to their fourth-floor apartment. Surprised to see him on the landing, she said, "What's happened?"

"Anne arrived a couple of hours ago, and I wanted to give you a few seconds, if you want it, to think about how you'd like to handle her before you come in."

Marta was glad to have that time to prepare, but she didn't express gratitude in words any more than she apologized after doing something inconsiderate, hurtful, or cruel. Putting gratitude or apology into words brought with it a burden of indebtedness that Marta refused to carry.

"How would you like me to help you deal with this?" Earl asked in a voice that was oily in its desire to please. He didn't like the fact that he was afraid of Marta.

"Deal with what?" Marta demanded.

"With Anne. You haven't spoken to her in two or three years, isn't that right?"

"Did she say why she's here, what she wants?"

"No, she gave no clue. She said she was afraid you wouldn't be happy about her showing up uninvited."

Marta picked up her book bag and trudged into the hallway of the apartment. As she put her things down and hung up her coat, the tension of the exchange with Earl on the landing gave way to that feeling of waiting for the main event to begin that was always in the wings for Marta. The place was dead quiet. Earl went to his bedroom and softly closed the door behind him.

Marta walked down to the end of the hallway and into the kitchen where she flopped down on one of the kitchen chairs. She let her flats drop to the floor, massaging her black stockinged feet with one hand, while with the other turning the pages of the morning newspaper spread out on the table in front of her. After about ten minutes, she got up and walked back up the hallway, first looking to her right into the empty living room and then knocking lightly on the door directly opposite, the door to the study. Marta could hear the desk chair scraping against the floor as Anne stood and came to the door. On opening the door, Anne found herself standing not two feet from her sister, a distance that felt uncomfortably close for both of them. Neither knew what to do: offer a handshake—too formal; a hug—too phony; a smile—obvious that it was strained. The awkward moment continued until Marta said, "It's been a long time. Let's go into the kitchen. You hungry? Want some coffee?"

"No, I'm fine."

Marta briskly turned to her left and walked the few steps into the kitchen, Anne trailing behind. Once in the kitchen, they took the same places at the table that they had at the family table as they grew up—at the long sides of the rectangular table across from one another.

Marta began, "What are you up to these days?"

"Thank you for starting. I was trying to think of how to start, but nothing seemed right. I don't know if you know that I left Uncle Bill and Aunt Ellen's place a year and a half ago, right after fulfilling the graduation requirements. I've been traveling around the country with a guy named Roger, picking up odd jobs, camping out, or living in motels. We got tired of that kind of life and we got tired of each other. There was never much between us. We just wanted company while we killed time waiting for some breeze to take us in one direction or another."

Marta said, "That sounds lonely."

"It was, and I'm glad it's over. What year are you in at State?"

"I'll be a senior in the fall."

"How's it been?" Anne asked, before interrupting herself. "What a ridiculous question. I'm so worried that I'm burdening you and that you would just as soon let our childhood die an early death, and me with it. I'm its ghost rising from the dead."

"That's true, but I have thought of you and hoped you were okay. Are you?"

"I'm okay now, and I can take care of myself. I hope you'll believe me when I say that. Otherwise you're going to think I'm dumping myself on your doorstep, which I'm not. If there's one thing I learned at home, it was how not to depend on others. You know that's true of me, don't you?"

"Yes, I do know that, and I do want to hear about what you've been doing since we last talked."

Neither Marta nor Anne knew whether Marta meant a word of what she said because, in truth, at that moment she wouldn't have minded if she never saw Anne again and never had another thought about their childhood. But Anne, who was burning to talk with the only other person in the world who knew what it was like to have grown up in their house, brushed aside her doubts about Marta's sincerity and unleashed a flood of words.

"All right, then I'll tell you the unedited or at least a less edited version of the last several years. Staying with Uncle Bill and Aunt Ellen for my senior year meant that I had to go to a different high school, which was hard, but it was worth it. Daddy—I hate using that name for him—got even worse after you went to live with Miss Saunders. He was furious that you had embarrassed him by moving in with her, but you were seventeen, so he couldn't do anything about it, and it saved him some money, which really sealed the deal for him. He continued to pinch my rear and brush against my breasts whenever he got the chance—the same stuff he was doing to you, and the other things too. Mom was pathetic and drank even more. She was useless. I'm afraid that this is just what you don't want to hear, so tell me when you've had enough. Last time we tried to talk we ended up arguing—I think because I was talking too much—and I don't want that to happen again."

"I don't picture you there when I think of that house," Marta said. "I've gotten good at shutting things out. No, I was always good at it. That was the difference between the two of us. I became cold, nothing could touch me. I know that the boys in high school used to call me icicle tits."

Anne drew in a breath of air sharply. "It hurts me to hear you say those words. I hoped you didn't know. They were animals."

"The only way to treat vicious animals is to scare them, and that's what I did, and I still do it. I scare Earl."

"You scare me too."

"I know."

"And I think I scare you," Anne said.

"You do."

"I have to talk about what went on at home," Anne said. "Please try to bear with me. It feels as if I have a machine inside of me that keeps churning out images that pile up until I get filled to the point of bursting. When I think of living there, I think of you sometimes. When the four of us were watching TV and he started doing that strange thing he did with his hand in his pocket, I remember looking over at you so that our eyes met and we'd roll our eyes about what he was doing. Sometimes you pretended not to notice I was trying to catch your eye."

"This is where I draw the line," Marta blurted out. "Don't start blaming me for your troubles. I had the same problems living in that house, and I did the best I could—we both did. But I couldn't carry you. I would have gone under if I'd tried, so I have no regrets about how I handled it. If I had to do it again, I would do exactly the same thing."

"Please don't get angry. I really don't blame you for any of it."

"You see. That's what I mean. When you say 'for any of it,' do you really hear no accusation in those words?"

"I guess there is."

"That's why you scare me—your accusations."

"We weren't just two boarders in the same house, Marta—it's hard for me to say your name too. I don't know why. You were a big part of my life, you still are. I don't know if you realize it, but you absorbed a lot of the radioactivity in that house in order to protect me. I'll never forget that regardless of how little I mean to you now."

"You're accusing me again."

"How can you say that? It's not an accusation to say that you protected me, and I feel grateful to you for it."

Marta said, "It feels like an accusation when you say that you don't matter much to me. I know I could have done more than I did for you, and I shouldn't have left you alone in that house with them."

"I wish you hadn't, but it was the right thing for you to do. And your moving out set the stage for me to move out for my senior year. It was more embarrassing to Daddy to have you live with someone outside of the family than to have me go to live with relatives. It looked like I was the problem, not them."

"I don't need to be appeased."

"But I need to tell you what happened—the whole thing. If I blame you for what happened, then I'm making up a story to make you feel bad, and that's not what I came here for. If that's what I end up doing, I'll have burned my bridges with you. I don't want that—for my own sake."

"I believe you, which sometimes is hard to do."

"I lie a lot. We both do—I lie by making up stories, you lie by omitting facts. At least that's what we did when we were growing up, and I still do it. I don't know whether you still do. You must have known that I was lying to you when I said that Roger and I ended our year of knocking around the country together because we got tired of one another. What happened was that I was having a hard time finishing high school while I was living at Uncle Bill and Aunt Ellen's, even though it was so much better there than being at home. They're very kind people. But I couldn't concentrate in school and even though there was nothing difficult about the classes I was taking, I couldn't study for exams, or even do homework. It was a gift that they let me graduate. The school even let me go a couple of months early to get me out, off their books. I thought that getting away from everything and everyone I knew would help. So I agreed to travel around the country with Roger.

"What really happened was that after about eight or ten weeks I began to fall apart. I couldn't sleep. I felt like I was on speed. I became convinced that Roger was trying to kill me. One night, after Roger was asleep, I took the car to get away from him—I thought that he was holding me captive. I was driving so fast and so much noise was raging in my head that I went off the road into a gulley and smashed the car up. When the police got there, I didn't know why I was there or what had happened, so they called an ambulance and had me taken to a hospital. I thought that they were locking me up under Roger's instructions."

Marta wondered whether Anne had been on drugs when she drove off the road, or if she had crashed the car in an attempt to kill herself, or whether, in fact, there ever was a car accident.

"Once we got to the ER, I tried to escape. They ended up strapping me down on a gurney. I had broken a rib, but other than that I was okay physically. I can't remember much of what happened in the hospital. They gave me medications to sedate me. When I woke up in the morning still strapped down, I was scared, but I could talk and behave in a way that allowed them to let me go instead of committing me. Please don't say anything to anyone about this. They contacted Daddy and Mom—I refuse to call them that anymore, so I'll just say 'father' and 'mother'—and they said that they weren't responsible for me or my expenses because I was eighteen then. They didn't ask to talk to me, which I'm glad about because I wouldn't have agreed to talk to them if they had. But there was no need for me to worry about that.

"I don't know what happened to Roger. I didn't see him again after that. He left my things at the front desk of the hospital. When I left the hospital, there was no place I particularly wanted to go, so without thinking much about it, I took a bus to New York City, and lived there for almost a year. It wasn't an easy life at all for the first couple of months. I'd meet someone at a club and sleep on their couch for a few nights and then find someone else to take me in for the next few nights. I got very lucky and was hired as a waitress at Gerde's Folk City, which was the place where the best of the new musicians played. I couldn't have afforded to pay to get in as a customer, but being a waitress was even better. I got to hear Bob Dylan sing songs he was trying out, songs that he hadn't recorded yet, and once or twice I got to say a few words to him after he sang. The atmosphere was electric night after night. The money I earned at Gerde's was enough to pay for a room in a flat in the East Village with a bunch of other kids my age."

There were so many embellishments in Anne's account that it was hard for her to remember the earlier parts of the story that she was telling so she could coordinate them with the later parts. Anne had in fact been committed for three days after the accident. Roger had helped get her out of the hospital after the involuntary commitment ended, and he looked after her for a couple of months after they arrived in New York. Anne didn't know why she didn't simply tell Marta the truth. The fabricated version just seemed to come out of her mouth.

Anne continued, "By the time I was in New York for nine or ten months, I began to find the pace of things exhausting, so I decided to move back to the town Aunt Ellen and Uncle Bill live in. I took a job at the bakery—you won't believe this, 'The Best of the Mid-West Bakery'—where I had worked after school and on weekends when I was in high school. I found a studio apartment near the bakery where I've been living since April."

Marta was becoming very uneasy. She had heard as much as she could take, and was tired of trying to figure out which parts of what Anne was saying were true.

Anne sat up with a start as if she had awakened from a dream. The room had darkened as the afternoon had drifted into evening. Anne was afraid that she had said far more than Marta wanted to hear, but at the same time, she didn't care—she had to tell her story to someone who knew her the way Marta did, even if she told it in the form of fictionalized accounts. Her stories, particularly those hardest to believe, contained the important truths of her life, not unlike the way the strangest of dreams do. Anne looked searchingly into Marta's face. Marta's eyes, although looking into hers, weren't quite meeting hers, and instead seemed to be focused on a spot an inch or two behind Anne's eyes.

Marta was interested in what Anne was saying, something that was rare for her when talking with anyone, including Earl. Until she had listened to Anne's soliloquy, Marta had entirely forgotten the role Anne had played in her life as a child. Marta liked to believe that she had been completely independent as she grew up and relied on no one, but she had relied heavily on Anne. It saddened her that she had cut Anne out of her life so ruthlessly two years earlier. Nonetheless, Marta was greatly relieved to hear that Anne had a job and an apartment of her own, and by implication, she was not asking Marta if she could move in with her and Earl.

The conversation then took on a lighter feel for both of them. They talked about how Marta never would have expected to be majoring in library science. She had always turned up her nose at the school librarians, viewing them as dried-up old maids.

"I didn't seek out books and libraries, they sought me out. For the 'work' part of the 'work-study program' here at State, I was assigned to library book repair, which as you can imagine, I wasn't thrilled about at first. It so happens that this backwater campus of the State University system has a 900,000-book library, which is the pride of the whole university. The library is housed in a huge building with more Greek columns than the Parthenon. The building bulges from both sides and from the rear as the original building has been expanded to house the rare book collection. The money to buy the rare books was donated by a tycoon who made his money starting what became the biggest supplier of chicken in the country.

"For the first two years I was strictly in the department that repairs the bindings of current books. There's quite a craft to it. I liked the meticulousness of the women who staffed the department—men are pretty much unwelcome by the staff, which is fine with me. The women there are a little like nuns, though they don't look up to men the way nuns look up to priests. The women at the library see their discipline as requiring a form of delicacy and refinement that is not in men's nature. They are very kind and encouraging to me, the first people in my life other than Miss Saunders who've taken a real interest in me. I love the feel of the bindings, the smell and texture of the paper, the different smells of the various acid-free adhesives. This may sound strange, but I'm not very interested in the contents of books—the stories, histories, theories. I like books not for what they contain, but as the physical thing itself, the thing you hold in your hands. I find books interesting as things in ways I can't describe. At the beginning of my junior year, they let me observe the restoration of the rare books. It was like being allowed into an operating room to watch open heart surgery. The pages of most of the rare books are so old that they'll disintegrate if you're at all imprecise in the way you handle them or if the humidity of the air is too high or too low. I'm sure I'm boring you. You go to New York City and I go to the library."

Anne had never before heard Marta talk with so much warmth in her voice. She credited this change to her relationship with Earl. The librarians were no doubt kind, but in the past Marta would have remained aloof.

Surprising herself with her own frankness, Marta said, "The fact that I'm living with Earl is also a surprise to me. Earl is not the kind of guy I imagined I'd be with, if I was to be with a guy at all. Even though I didn't like the flashy, cocksure type in high school, I somehow expected that I'd end up with one. I don't know why. Earl is the first guy I ever really dated. I tried to push Earl away for a long time when he was trying to strike up conversations with me. I liked the fact that he didn't give up, even when I was being terribly rude to him—pretending not to see him, or worse yet, pretending not to even recognize him if our paths crossed on the quad or in a hallway. I was awful to him. He's unlike any other person I've met. He knows how to talk honestly—that's what I like most about him, even though I don't join him in that kind of talk. Even now, I take things very slowly with him. I think I scare him sometimes— I know I scare him sometimes because I try to. I want things to remain undefined between us. We're living together, but that's not a promise to marry him or even to continue to be with him next week or next semester."

Just as Marta had not interrupted or asked questions when Anne was talking, Anne did the same for Marta. Like Marta, Anne had a good many thoughts while Marta spoke. Anne felt glimmers of softness in Marta that she had never seen before, and the beginnings, but only the beginnings, of real strength, as opposed to toughness. Marta was still scared to death of talking about life at home while they were growing up, but to her credit, Marta hadn't become distraught, as she had in the past, when Anne made reference to the family. Most important to Anne was the fact that she saw in Marta inklings of the big sister she once knew, who had protected her as best she could, a big sister whom Anne had given up for dead.

The conversation returned to Marta's college courses.

"I hated every day of school in junior high and high school, but I actually enjoy my classes here. I'm not bored and I don't feel stupid. It would be even more exciting for you because you're a lot smarter than I am."

"I am not," Anne said definitively and sincerely.

"You've always been able to understand things that just confuse me," Marta said.

"Like what?"

"Oh, you know. When we used to watch detective shows or spy shows on TV, I was always asking you to explain what was happening—who was on whose side, were these the same people at a different time in their lives, and sometimes I'd just say, 'Who are these people?' and you'd laugh and then I'd laugh because you were three years younger and I was asking you."

"But, Marta, you understood the important things."

"Like what?"

"Important things like not to be fooled when he was acting 'fatherly,' not to believe him when he told mother he was sorry and would never hit her again, and not to believe her when she said she'd take us and leave him if he ever hit her again."

73

Marta's eyes met Anne's in frightened knowing, a form of communication they had often used as children.

Anne changed the topic without appearing to do so by saying, "I could never pass a college course, much less do as well as you have. To do what you're doing you have be able to concentrate on something until it unfolds itself in front of you. I couldn't even do that in high school."

Marta disagreed. "I know how smart you are. I was proud of you when we were kids because you were so much smarter than any of the other kids, even the kids my age."

It was not lost to either Marta or Anne that Marta herself had brought up something from childhood, but neither of them was foolish enough to let on that she noticed.

Earl knocked on the edge of the kitchen door jam and asked if Anne and Marta wanted to go out to the local restaurant where he and Marta went when they didn't feel like cooking. The fact that a man had appeared in the room felt somehow unreal to both Marta and Anne. Even if he'd been eavesdropping during their entire conversation, he could not have understood a word of what they were saying.

SIX

Warren, sitting up in bed in the semi-darkness, staring at the shadows on the opposite wall, asked Melody, "What's a coroner?"

Melody answered, "I asked Daddy that and he said it's a doctor who examines dead bodies to see what they died of. They want to see if someone killed her."

"They already know Daddy killed her. He's told them that himself."

"But they want to find out if he did it on purpose," she said.

"He was trying to stop her from stabbing me."

"Warren, the deputy keeps trying to get Daddy to say that he didn't have to kill her to protect us or himself. He could have just pushed her or held her instead of hitting her so hard she went flying and broke her neck."

"Do you think he did it on purpose?"

"No," Melody said with finality.

"The doctor must think there's a chance he wanted to kill her—he said the funeral had to be set back for two days so he could take more time examining the body, didn't he?"

"Yeah. I don't know what they're thinking. They like to turn things into a murder investigation—it makes them feel like detectives in the movies," Melody said.

Warren and Melody were quiet for a while as they mulled over the question of whether their father had murdered their mother—Melody's using the word murder had scared both of them.

"You're going to think I'm being stupid," Melody said, "but it's something that's serious for me, so don't laugh at me. I mean it."

"I won't."

"For a funeral you're supposed to wear a black dress, and I don't have one. I only have one dress and it's too small for me and it's a pale yellow cotton print dress with small, dark green birds all over it. Daddy wouldn't know what I was talking about if I told him I need a black dress for the funeral. One of the only things *she* was good at was making clothes look better than they really were. She might have sewn something black onto my yellow dress or made a black sash for it, or something."

Warren thought he heard Melody crying, but he didn't turn to see if she was.

He asked, "Can't you make something black for the dress, like a sash or something?"

"I don't know how to sew that well. *She* wanted to teach me but I made believe I couldn't do it. She gave up after a while."

Melody was right, of course, to think that the deputy sheriff suspected Earl of intentionally killing Marta. The following day, Randy said to his boss, "There's something that makes no sense at all. Earl won't say that his wife was out of her mind about the boy's thumb sucking and tried to stab his hand with a knife. The girl's story is perfectly believable and Earl showed us where the gloves and leather shoelaces were kept. He refuses to say that two and two make four. It's as if he's intent on going to his grave or possibly to prison

76

with a secret that is no longer secret. Who does he think he's protecting—his wife who's dead? Or his children, from what? Or himself—what's he hiding that could be worth getting arrested for, not that we have enough to arrest him for anything."

Melody decided that the only person she could turn to for advice about how to alter her yellow print dress was her schoolteacher, Miss Wells. She was by no means an obvious choice because she was old, by Melody's standards, and plump and frumpy, and she seemed not to be aware that there existed a category called "stylish clothes." Melody, a couple of years earlier, had begun to notice what people were wearing in the magazines on the racks in the pharmacy and the grocery store. Melody was particularly interested in the photographs and stories about movie stars and their romances. These magazines were filled with ads in which beautiful women modeled clothes that Melody at first found hard to believe that real people actually wore in public. Some of the dresses were so low cut in front that you could see the bare roundness of the inner side of both of the women's breasts, and some of the dresses hardly had anything covering the backs of the models. Melody was as excited as she was shocked and amazed. It was a very long way from the world of these magazines to the world Melody inhabited, and even further light years to whatever it was that Miss Wells' "style" might be. Despite this, Melody felt certain that every woman she knew, other than Miss Wells, would disdainfully wave her off and mutter to anyone who happened to be around that Melody had turned out shamelessly vain. Melody would have called her grandmother if she were still alive.

Melody spent most of the night deliberating about how to approach Miss Wells. The following morning, after her chores were done, she rode her bike to school with a shoe box balanced on the handlebars. She arrived at the school building at around ten and was surprised to see the school parking lot half-filled with cars and vans even though school would not be starting for another week or so. Before going in, Melody carefully tucked her bike along with the shoe box under the clot of low branches of an ancient-looking pine tree.

The recently constructed one-storey brick school building had a modern L-shape design. The desk of the school secretary, Laurel Marshall, was positioned in such a way that she was facing a plate glass window with a sliding glass pane, which separated her office from the corridor just inside the front doors of the school. Miss Marshall had heard that Marta Bromfman had died under terrible circumstances involving a knife attack and a brutal fight between the physically mismatched Marta and Earl that ended in Marta's death by means of a broken neck. To make matters all the more tragic, Melody and Warren had been within feet of their mother when her neck was broken. When Miss Marshall saw Melody come through the front doors, she knocked hard on the sliding glass window separating her from Melody, and when she got the attention of the girl, she motioned her to come into the office to talk to her.

Melody was disappointed to have been spotted by Miss Marshall. She did not want to talk to Miss Marshall about anything, and in particular, did not want to talk about her mother's death. Once in the office, Melody decided to take the lead in the conversation by saying that she had come to see Miss Wells and wondered if she had come in yet.

Miss Marshall said, "I haven't seen her today, sweetie, but she's been in every day this week getting her classroom ready for the new term."

Before Miss Marshall could go on, Melody said, "Let me run down to her classroom to see if she got here while you were doing something."

With that, Melody dashed out into the hallway, which was crowned by bulbous plastic skylights. She walked quickly down to Miss Wells' room, only to find it empty. Melody

78

looked around for a few minutes before reluctantly returning to Miss Marshall's desk.

"You were right. She's not there or anywhere else in the building," Melody said.

With an understanding smile, Miss Marshall said, "I've called Miss Wells at her home and she said that she'd be here within the hour. I hope it's all right that I told her that you were here and wanted to talk to her."

Melody said, "Thank you. That was awfully nice of you to do," and she meant it.

"You're welcome to sit here with me until Miss Wells gets here, unless you'd like to go outside."

"I think I'll go outside and ride my bike, but thanks for what you did."

When Miss Wells drove into the school lot, Melody grabbed her shoe box, scrambled out from her cool, dark, fragrant spot under the pine tree, and ran to meet Miss Wells as she got out of her car.

Once in Miss Wells' classroom, Melody opened her shoe box, lifted the folded fabric with both hands, and let the thin yellow dress unfurl in front of her. Miss Wells took the dress from Melody and spread it out on her desk.

Melody explained, "You probably know, but my mother died on Tuesday, and her funeral is going to be on Saturday or Sunday. All I have to wear is this dress, which is not dark enough for a funeral and it needs altering because it's too small for me now."

Melody told Miss Wells her idea about adding a black sash. Miss Wells said to Melody that she must have looked very pretty in this dress at one time, but unfortunately the dress had not grown up while Melody had. She asked Melody if she had time to take a drive with her to a neighboring town where there was a clothing shop in which she thought they could find something for Melody to wear to the funeral. Melody sputtered that she only had a few dollars saved up. Miss Wells, acting as if she hadn't heard Melody, ushered her to the parking lot. It took about forty-five minutes to drive to the clothing store. Miss Wells tuned the radio to a popular music station because she could tell that Melody didn't know what to say.

The store was unlike any store Melody had ever been in. There were tables with fall sweaters, racks of summer dresses that were on sale, and other racks of the new fall dresses. Brightly lit glass display cases were filled with sparkling earrings and bracelets, many made of silver and gold, but others made of very small seashells or jewels hanging on a slender strand of silver. Melody tried not to stare at these treasure chests.

Miss Wells walked Melody to the back of the store where there was a mirror with three panels on it so you could see yourself from three directions. A saleslady followed them very quietly and discreetly.

Miss Wells said to the saleslady, "This is Melody. She had a very sad thing happen this week. Her mother died and we're here to find a dress that will be right for her to wear at the funeral."

The saleslady said, "Melody, I'm very sorry to hear that your mother died. It's a very hard thing to bear. I lost my mother a few years ago and even though I'm a grown woman, I felt like a small child without her, and still do in a lot of ways. I can't imagine what it's like for you at your age to lose your mother."

Even though Melody knew that the effect of her mother's death was nothing like what the saleslady imagined, she appreciated her talking to her in such a respectful way, and not treating her as a little girl.

"I'd suggest a solid color dress—a dark color, maybe dark blue or dark green, or perhaps even black, but black might be too old and heavy for a beautiful young woman like you. Let me see what we have in your size. Since it's still summer, we're restricted to light fabrics, probably cotton or silk, but most summer dresses are neither solid colored nor dark. But the fortunate side of that coin is that those that are a dark solid color are likely to be the dresses that haven't been sold yet. I'll try to find something suitable for you to look at, and we can take it from there."

After more than an hour of trying on dresses, Melody, Miss Wells, and the saleslady all agreed on a dark blue, cotton dress on which a black paisley pattern was very subtly printed. It was meant to be an evening dress, but the high neck, short sleeves, and loose, flowing lines of the dress made it an appropriate dress for a funeral. Melody was stunned and very, very pleased by what she saw when she looked in the mirror. Miss Wells insisted that Melody buy black satin flats to go with the dress.

In the car, on their way back to the school, Melody wept in response to the extraordinary kindness Miss Wells had shown her.

That night, Earl, as he so often did, sat in the armchair in the corner of the first floor room listening to the children talking in their room after they'd gone to bed. The sound of their voices, but not the words, filtered down through the floor—talk, now fervent, now earnest, now silly, now deadly serious. He was glad that he could not make out the words—he could savor the soothing music of their voices without fear of eavesdropping. When they finally went off to sleep, Earl sat thinking or listening to the radio, wrapped in the dim light of the table lamp next to his chair.

As Earl sat there after the children had fallen asleep, it seemed to him that that first weekend when he had met Anne, all those years ago, had marked the beginning of a torrent of events that would shape the remainder of his life and the lives of Marta and Anne. It struck him how very young he had been, and how very young Marta and Anne had been, as those events began to unfold—Anne was eighteen, he was twenty, and Marta had just turned twenty-one. They hadn't felt young at the time, which is always the case for young people, he supposed. As Earl was thinking these thoughts, he was thirty-six, which did not seem young to him. He felt quite old, and tired.

When he, along with Marta and Anne, returned to the attic apartment after dinner the first evening of Anne's unexpected arrival, Marta invited Anne to stay for the remainder of the weekend. Anne protested that she did not want to impose on Marta and Earl, but Marta insisted. After Anne left to take the bus back to her apartment on Sunday afternoon, both Marta and Earl felt her absence, each in their own way. Marta had not recognized before Anne's visit that Anne had been the only friend that she'd ever had, and that she had been terribly lonely not only during the two years that they had not spoken, but also during the year after she moved out of their parents' house to live with Miss Saunders. Because she and Anne had been living in fear so much of the time while they were living together at home, they felt more like allies—underground collaborators—than like friends or even sisters, at least that's how Marta saw it as she looked back on it. But she increasingly doubted her own judgment about anything having to do with feelings, knowing how easy it was for her to be contemptuous of people who, it seemed to her, made romantic stories of their lives and the people in them. She was repelled by such fictions.

Marta felt more distant from Earl during and after Anne's first visit. She was annoyed with him for occupying space, for breathing, for the way he held his fork and the way he chewed his food. She had always liked the fact that he was not like other men. He was not a loud, beer-drinking, slap-on-the-back, vulgar lunk, which was how she saw almost all of the other male students at the university, and a good many of the male faculty. But now Earl was beginning to grate on her because he was not entirely free of those qualities. The fact that he was tall and muscular and a football player now irritated her.

82

Buzzing and churning in Earl, with all the throbbing intensity of one of the hornets' nests that he and his friends had punctured with sticks when he was a boy, were the continuing effects of his first exchange with Anne on the landing outside the apartment. He had never before experienced anything remotely like that feeling. After only the first few words had been exchanged between them, the thought went through his head that people don't choose when to fall in love, and they don't choose whom to fall in love with. Why had no one ever told him that the most important thing in your life will be something that happens to you, and you will not have a say in the matter? His feeling of being in love seemed to gain momentum by the minute. He felt as if he was driving a car with the accelerator pressed to the floor, and he could not release it. That he had fallen in love with Marta's sister felt to him like a cruel joke played by fate.

Earl vowed to himself again and again as it was happening and in the days that followed that he would keep his distance—both literally and figuratively—from Anne because the outcome of falling in love with her could only be disastrous for him and Marta. But he could only manage to keep that vow for a few seconds before a fresh wave of excitement swept through him. He found Anne to be far more beautiful than Marta, not because of individual physical features, but because of the spark he saw in Anne's eyes. Not only that, everything about her was sexy—the way she looked at him with her green eyes flecked with gold, the softness of her lips, the sound of her voice which made him feel as if she were squeezing his arm with each word she spoke, the way her whole body moved as she stood talking, her way of interrupting herself with humorous, self-effacing remarks that kept her sexiness understated and all the more alluring. Marta was very pretty, but she was not sexy. When Earl was with Anne, he had to restrain himself from staring at her in disbelief that a creature as beautiful as this was there in the same room with him and he was talking to her.

83

The pain of the almost unbearable attraction that he felt for Anne was compounded by the torment of self-doubt. Was he making a fool of himself as he gawked at her like a pathetic schoolboy looking dreamily at his teacher? Did she even notice him? Was he only a forgettable minor character, the doorman in the real story, which was the story of sisters reuniting after a long estrangement? How could he be so stupid as to believe that she had fallen in love with him? But he not only hoped that that was so, he could not stop himself from believing it—based on what? Based on nothing. She's a flirt and is this way with every guy she meets. She knows she is irresistibly sexy and uses that to get guys to go crazy for her, and then she goes on with her life leaving the poor slobs to die of heartbreak. But that was not the girl he had spoken with. She was not a hardened, self-assured tease. Quite the contrary. She seemed like a waif when she was standing on the landing asking to come in to a place where she was afraid she was unwelcome. For Earl, the combination of these qualities was wondrous. He had been surprised that a girl as pretty as Marta would give him the time of day—which, of course, she had not given him for a long time. But that was different. In the beginning, he never cared all that much for her as a person. He wanted a pretty girl to make out with. He had not fallen in love with her. He grew to like her and to enjoy spending time with her, although never without feeling afraid of her wrath, which could at any moment be unleashed with the force of the collision of tectonic plates. In the time that they had been together, Earl had become very protective of Marta as he came to realize how fragile she was. Before he met Anne, he had felt that he was protecting Marta from herself—from her self-loathing—but now he felt he was protecting her from his own disloyalty.

Even though Marta and Earl found one another to be an encumbrance after Anne's first visit, neither wanted to do anything to upset the status quo that they had established. Marta invited Anne to spend the next weekend with them, but

Anne had to work that Saturday at the bakery, and could not make it until the following weekend.

Both Marta and Earl looked forward to Anne's next visit, but each was afraid that the spell Anne had cast would be broken. The welcome Anne received when she arrived for her second visit felt strained to all three of them. It was very difficult to find the right tone of voice, the right words, the right physical behavior for this second reunion—"Glad to see you," "How've you been?" a hug, a pat on the arm, an offer to carry her knapsack—nothing felt right to any of them. Earl tried not to appear like a puppy dog eagerly awaiting the children's return from school. Marta tried to appear at ease, a state that was entirely foreign to her. And Anne did what she could to hide her fear that Marta would find her a constant reminder of childhood, and again banish her. Over dinner they managed to simulate enjoyment of one another. Earl and Marta both wished they had Anne to themselves, but at the same time were relieved that the other was there to save the evening from becoming a complete disaster. By the end of the weekend, they were all tired and disappointed.

Anne was not only shaken by the tension of the visit, she was possessed by a need to fix it. The twelve days separating this visit from the next seemed like months. She repeatedly went over in her mind each of the conversations she had with Marta, second-guessing everything that she had said. She was afraid that she had given the appearance of a pathetic younger sister who would, if given the chance, live parasitically off of the family that Marta and Earl had made for themselves. What she had said to Marta about her time in New York City had been true to an extent, but she had edited out the fact that she had eaten out of dumpsters. She and Roger were not artists trying to bring their work to the attention of the world—they were hangers-on. There was only a thin line between them and the derelicts and prostitutes living on the streets and in the buildings of Avenue C. Roger's "friends"

85

were merely names he had been given of acquaintances of people he had met in bars. She and Roger slept on floors of dingy apartments. Sex with male "hosts" was often expected, and she provided it. Drugs were everywhere and Anne, desperate to be accepted, smoked a lot of pot and dabbled in quaalude and cocaine.

The "music scene" in New York, as Anne had experienced it, was a deadly serious game of making yourself known by attaching yourself to the better-known musicians and then promoting yourself through endless self-aggrandizement in the form of dropping the names of the people for whom you had played back-up.

She had not waitressed at Gerde's Folk City, as she had told Marta—the club didn't have waiters or waitresses, just a walk-up bar. She hadn't even been part of the clean-up crew there. Most of the work she was able to get was temping as a file clerk and occasionally as a typist at large and small businesses in Manhattan. She did not have the clothes, accessories, make-up, or the stylish, clean shiny hair that was expected. The jobs did not last long, and more often than not, she was treated as if she exuded a foul odor. Once, the first morning she showed up for an office job, the female manager took one look at her, paid her for a day's work, and told her to leave.

But despite the myriad forms of degradation in which Anne took part, she knew that this was not being imposed on her—no one had asked her to live the life she was living in New York, and certainly no one was keeping her there. She had to remind herself that she genuinely did love the music she heard during her year in New York. Was she lying to herself about the redeeming parts of that year? Not entirely, she hoped. With the money Anne made temping, and the money spent on her by men she was seeing, she was able to go to the clubs and cafés to hear the music that was becoming part of her. With the little bit of money she could spare, she bought albums and singles, mostly used and some pirated, which she sent to her aunt and uncle to keep for her until she got back. This much was true, she said to herself.

Anne knocked on the door of the attic apartment on a Friday afternoon two weeks after the disappointing second visit. Earl answered the door, Marta was out. Anne trucked past Earl, barely saying a word, heading for the living room. She was loaded down, carrying in her right hand what looked to Earl to be a hard, tan typewriter case, and in her left hand, an over-filled plastic shopping bag containing sharp-edged objects that were on the verge of cutting through the bag in a dozen places. Once in the living room, Anne wordlessly set to work like a surgeon laying out her instruments on the rectangular table between the two windows on the far wall. Earl watched silently from the threshold of the room. The hard, box-like thing was a turntable with speakers built into the sides of the case. Anne uncoiled the brown electrical cord that lay droopily on the turntable and plugged it into the wall socket in the baseboard under the table.

She carefully removed from the shopping bag, one by one, a pile of eight or ten well-worn 33-rpm record albums and a handful of 45-rpm singles in white paper sheaths, placing them in two neat stacks on the table to the left of the turntable. Using two hands to tenderly thumb through the albums, she found the one that she was looking for and placed it on the top of the pile. Anne pulled a straight-backed wooden chair with a cushioned seat to a position a few feet from the record player. She motioned Earl to place the matching chair opposite hers.

Pointing to the stacks of records, Anne said, "This, Earl, is the Holy Grail of contemporary music, music you've probably never heard, and I doubt you'll like much of it when you do hear it. In fact I hope you don't like any of it right away because it should feel off or not right, not what you were hoping for. You may have to listen to it five or ten times before you'll be able to hear in it something that's not only new and unfamiliar, but powerfully, even violently, right. I told Marta, and I don't know if she's told you, but I spent a year in New York City, the first months of which I was half out of my mind—and the rest of that time I was fully out of my mind. The guy I was with was worthless in most ways. He had the names of quite a few people in the Alphabet Avenues of the East Village, which are pretty slummy parts of the city. Not infrequently we ate out of dumpsters and slept on the floor of buildings under construction. Don't fool yourself about any of that being glamorous, it wasn't. It's awful to feel like a derelict."

Earl had to smile inwardly because, as sexy as she was, Anne had looked more than a little like a bag lady as she trudged through the apartment loaded down with her possessions.

Anne continued to speak in her faux drill sergeant way. "That way of living—more subsisting than living—was partially offset by the fact that the guy I was with really knew music and he knew where to find the people who were good musicians, some of them great musicians. It took me time to hear what he heard. When we were at a club, he once leaned over and said to me, 'Listen to the way he gets that saxophone to sing like a gravel-throated old man,' and another time he said, 'Listen to the way he gets the trumpet to sound like a woman screaming into the desert night. No one else in the world can do that with a trumpet.'"

Anne took a breath and asked, "Do you listen to music, Earl?"

"Yeah, on the radio. I don't buy records."

"Who do you like?"

"I guess I like some songs that aren't cool, but I like them. I like Johnny Cash, Jimmy Dean, Patsy Cline. Are they really bad to like?" Earl said chidingly.

"No, they're not bad to like, but, with the possible exception of Patsy Cline, they're singers that your parents' generation would like too, and you haven't heard the music that our generation is making. It's music that is impossible for your parents to like, and most of their music is impossible for us to like. In fact, I hate their music—Duke Ellington bores me to death and Frank Sinatra's unctuous voice makes my skin crawl. My mother forbade us to say a word while a Perry Como song was being played on the radio. Johnny Cash is okay, but he's not reinventing music, he's playing around with the old stuff. Our music wasn't made for our parents and no one in their generation could have made it. The next generation won't like our music the way we do, and we won't like theirs—we won't really understand it."

"You think it's too late for me?"

"We'll have to see. I'm not going to start you off easy by playing someone like Joan Baez who sings nice folk songs that our parents wouldn't mind listening to, although they wouldn't hear in it what we hear. I'm going to make a big leap here, so don't worry if you don't like it," she said as she shook the record out of the album jacket she had found earlier. "The voice isn't pretty, and it's not trying to be. The song I'm going to play is called 'Don't Think Twice, It's All Right.'"

She gently placed the needle on one of the inner tracks. The sound from the turntable speakers was thin and crackly.

This song was a shocker for Earl. Anne was right, he had never heard anything remotely like it. At first he hated it, but by the end he wasn't sure what he thought.

He said, "Play that again."

They listened and he laughed out loud after the line in which Dylan used the word "know'd" to rhyme with "road." The song was about breaking up with a girl, but it was not a song about heartbreak, which seemed to be the only subject country music was about. Earl enjoyed the lyrics. The singer was unapologetically bitter about how he'd been treated, but he wasn't feeling sorry for himself—that would have given too much credit to the girl he was breaking up with. He was ironic, and the heavy rhyming made the irony genuinely funny in a self-mocking way. The music was good, very good. Earl asked to hear it a third time. After the song was over, Anne gently placed the arm of the record player back on its stand. Earl was speechless for half a minute.

He then said, "You're going to think I'm saying this just to impress you, but I'm not. I love that song."

Anne said, "I like it too. I heard Dylan trying it out at Gerde's Folk City, a club in Greenwich Village. I waitressed and cleaned the place after the shows at Gerde's so I could listen to the music. Dylan looked just like he does here on the album cover. Unlike a lot of the other singers, he stayed to himself. He slipped out of the back of the club when he was done, not saying anything to anybody."

Although Anne had not worked at Gerde's, she had been there quite a few times and had in fact heard Dylan sing that song.

Anne talked about crossover music, gospel, rhythm and blues, soul music, and the names of a lot of Negro singers. The only one of these singers that Earl had heard of was Louis Armstrong. Earl's mind wandered. Some of his football teammates at the university were Negroes, but they tended to form a group of their own. Earl was too shy or frightened to approach them, and he figured they probably felt the same about him and the rest of the whites on the team. Earl was eight or nine years old the first time he saw a Negro man on television. He was alarmed by what had happened to the man's skin. He ran to his mother to tell her what he'd seen. As he thought back on it, Earl felt proud of the way his mother had explained that the man he had seen on television was a Negro man, and that Negroes were people who were just the same as herself and Earl and everyone else. She said that in parts of this country Negroes used to be owned as slaves and that even then—it must have been around 1950, Earl guessed—Negroes in parts of this country still weren't allowed to eat where white people ate and had to sit in the back of movie theaters and buses. She said that it made her feel like saying to people who did that to other people, "Shame on you, shame on you."

Earl was jarred by the way Anne pulled the needle of the record player from the Wilson Pickett single she was playing the moment it ended.

She said, "Now I'm going to try you out on some jazz. The jazz world is a whole different world."

Anne could feel her mind speeding up. What had earlier felt like a personal gift to Earl was now beginning to feel like a performance she could not stop. She didn't like the feeling, but she was in its grip. Earl sensed the change in Anne and suggested that they take a break. Anne ignored what Earl said as she thumbed briskly through her stack of albums and pulled out *Kind of Blue*.

She explained, "When they recorded this, Miles Davis, the lead trumpet player, didn't tell the other musicians in the group what they were going to play. He had some ideas ahead of time, but nothing solid. He started off and the others immediately picked up on what he was doing. They each waited for the right moment to take the lead, and let the others talk back to him with their instruments. What you're going to hear on this record is their first time playing each cut. They couldn't play it the same way again if they tried, and they wouldn't want to. That's what jazz is. It's improvisation of a particular kind—it's pure music making itself up as it goes. There are jazz clubs in Harlem where hardly any white people go. And some theaters too. I went with some Negro friends to the Apollo Theater to see James Brown. I was the only white person there. The Savoy Ball Room, on the edge of Harlem, was a place of its own. It could hold 5,000 people. I saw Junior Walker and the All-Stars doing 'Shotgun' and some other acts I can't remember. The crowd there was very tough on the acts and would boo and jeer them off stage after thirty seconds if they didn't measure up."

In truth, she had never been to the Apollo or to any of the other Harlem theaters or jazz clubs, but in her current state of mind, she felt that she had frequented these places.

Anne placed the needle on the outermost groove of *Kind of Blue*, sat down in her chair, closed her eyes, and let her arms go loose at her sides. Earl closed his eyes too. The tension drained from the room as they listened silently for a long time, maybe half an hour, maybe more. The spell was shattered when the front door of the apartment slammed shut and footsteps made their way down the hallway. Marta looked into the living room and saw that the room had been transformed. The music she heard was that highbrow stuff you're supposed to like, but you really don't. She and Earl had never owned a record player. Earl listened to music on the radio, Marta did not. There were albums all over the place, some stacked next to the record player, some strewn on the floor between Earl and Anne. The two of them might as well have been holding up a sign saying, "PRIVATE. MEMBERS ONLY." She stood there silently, her face awash with pain. She had been caught off guard, a state of affairs that she had spent most of her life trying to prevent.

Without a whiff of apology, Anne calmly said, "Marta, I've played Earl some music from records I brought back from New York, things they don't play on the radio out here. When I was here last time, I thought that everything I said or did went flat. I was afraid that I was a burden for the two of you, so I brought something that I hoped would help earn my keep. What I learned about music in New York is the only thing that's interesting about me, so I brought some of it."

Marta, glaring at Anne, said, "You're good at playing with the truth—*you* know that and *I* know that. Do you think I'm a moron?

"Marta, please believe me that I don't want to leave you out or steal Earl away from you. I took a big risk coming here unannounced a few weeks ago. You could have humiliated me by telling me to leave and never bother you again. You're the only reason I'm here. I hope you know that that's true. I realize that this may not be believable to you, but I so looked forward to playing this music for you that I couldn't wait till you got home. I should have waited for you."

Despite the fact Marta believed Anne, she couldn't refrain from responding venomously. "You talk too much. You can't stop talking, can you?"

Even as Marta was saying these words, she was afraid that she was destroying something that she wanted very badly to preserve. She knew that Earl's capacity to put up with her bitterness was almost endless, but she didn't know how much of it Anne could take.

Anne said, "I know that this looks as if I'm trying to woo Earl by serenading him with music. I'd think that too if I were to walk in on us. But I'm not looking for a boyfriend, I'm looking for what you and I had before. I came with my music this time because I thought that it would give me a way of being a real, living person here, and not a ghost from a past you'd like to forget. How do you talk to a ghost? You don't. You just try to get rid of it and return to real life in the present."

Marta was silent for a little while. Earl tried to disappear by remaining absolutely still. Anne, awaiting Marta's verdict, felt that what she had said was true—she hoped it was true.

Marta finally said, "I believe you, but I hope I'm not making a mistake."

Anne said nervously, "I do talk too much when I'm afraid. I don't know what's going to come out of my mouth. I'm sorry that you had to pay the price for it this time. I won't make a fuss if you tell me to leave and not come back."

None of them slept well that night. In the morning, it was clear from Marta's demeanor—even before she said a word—that she had stepped back from the brink of an outburst of righteous indignation that would have brought an end to Anne's attempt to repair things between the two of them.

Later that morning, Anne said to Marta, "I don't know if there will ever be a right time for this after what happened yesterday, but I would love to listen with you to some of the music I heard in New York. It would mean a lot to me."

Marta said, "Okay."

As the two of them went into the living room, they could hear Earl leaving the apartment. Anne spoke in a very different way from the way she had spoken to Earl. She knew that Marta was scared that she would not get it, frightened that she was so shut off from the world and from herself that she would not be able to understand Anne's music and would feel stupid, as she so often did. Anne, too, was frightened that things would go terribly wrong. She did not want to play the music for Marta in the way she did for Earl. She cringed as she recalled the way she had initially played the role with Earl of the tough, knowledgeable, demanding teacher, who, underneath it all, has a good heart and only wants what's best for her students. She had become increasingly out of control and now felt deeply embarrassed by it.

Anne patiently and tenderly told Marta stories of the singers whose music she was going to play and told her what was new about these songs and what she particularly liked about each of them. She felt no inclination to engage either in name dropping or in portraying herself as somebody other than who she had been in New York: a directionless girl, fresh out of high school, who came to love the music being performed by people whom she did not know and who had no use for her. The first album that Anne took from her plastic shopping bag was Billie Holiday's *Lady Sings the Blues*.

Anne said, "I'm going to begin with a song by the singer whose music helped me survive my year in New York. She died four years before I got there. Her name is Billie Holiday. When I listened to her songs, I felt less alone."

"What did she die of?"

"She died at forty-four of alcoholism. As you'll hear in her voice, she lived a very sad life, but her singing that sadness comforted me. I don't know why, but it did. It was a terrible year for me, the culmination of many terrible years. I don't have to explain it to you. I'm going to shut up and let you hear the song, 'Willow Weep for Me.'"

Anne was surprised to see tears on Marta's cheeks as she listened to the song. Anne had never before seen Marta cry. They then listened to a single, Nina Simone's "I Love You Porgy." Anne didn't play any of Dylan's songs because she thought that male irony just didn't suit Marta. Neither did Anne play anything by Miles Davis, whose music seemed too abstract for Marta. Marta asked Anne to play more of *Lady Sings the Blues*. She was still and silent as they listened to every cut on both sides of the album. Marta had never heard of any of the singers that Anne played, nor had she heard anything remotely related to the sound of the songs being sung, but to her surprise, this did not make her feel stupid and backward. It made her feel full.

SEVEN

Randy had asked Earl whether he would like to be the one to inform Marta's parents of her death, adding that he was going to have to talk to them to complete the Sheriff's Department "paperwork" connected with her death. Earl said that it would be fine with him if Randy let them know. He said that he had never met them and didn't know if they were still living in the same small town in the western part of the state where Marta grew up.

Two days later Randy told Earl that he had spoken to Marta's father who said he was sorry to receive the news, but the journey would be too taxing for him and Marta's mother. He said that Marta's older brother was living somewhere in upstate New York, but they had not heard from him in years. They also said that they had lost contact with Marta's younger sister, and did not even know if she was still alive. Randy said that it struck him as odd that Marta's father included in his response the possibility that his younger daughter was dead. She was only in her early thirties. Melody and Warren had never met their mother's parents, nor did they know that she had a sister and brother.

When Earl called the various members of his family to tell them that Marta had died, he asked them not to trouble themselves with the long trip. All the members of his family, including his father, told him that they would like to be at the funeral, but Earl said that while he appreciated their wish to be there, in truth, he was trying to keep things as simple as possible so he could tend to the practical matters of the funeral, taking care of the children, and completing the harvest.

The coroner's report was filed with the county the day before Marta's funeral. In the report, Dr. Raymond Westin concluded that Marta "had been killed by the impact of a blunt object, probably someone's shoulder, on the deceased's upper body and neck, which was so forceful as to not only shatter every bone in the cervical and upper lumbar spine, but also to completely sever the spinal cord, trachea, esophagus, and all the major blood vessels in the neck, which pulled the brainstem down into the sub-cranial space created by the massive dislocation of internal structures. Marta Bromfman died instantly on impact; the collision with the floor was not a cause of death."

Marta's funeral was held at the United Methodist church on Tolliver Street five days after she died. She would have been livid had she known about this, for as Earl was well aware, she had an extreme distaste for religion of any sort. But Earl decided that Marta no longer had a say in the matter. Even though Earl himself was not a believer and had not attended church since he was in high school, he thought it would be insulting to his family and to his friends in town not to have a church funeral at the Methodist church, a place that had been important to his parents and grandparents.

The church was small—only fifty or sixty feet from the entry door to the altar—with six large, clear windows on each side, which let in sunlight filtered through the large oaks and maples on the west side of the church and the towering cottonwoods on the east. Earl, Warren, and Melody sat at the end of the first row of pews nearest the central aisle. Marta's pine casket lay open at the front of the church with several arrangements of chrysanthemums, lilies, and glads beside it.

Earl got up to spend a little time standing next to the casket as the funeral guests slowly made their way in. Marta looked in death very much the way she had in life. The sallow skin of her face was stretched tightly across her cheekbones in such a way that her lips were pulled to the sides, giving the impression of restrained impatience. Earl wished he missed her, but he didn't. He felt sorry for her. Practically from the time they first met he had tried to show her that there was no need to feel frightened of him, and no need to frighten him away. Her adult life, as well as her life as a child, was almost entirely devoid of warmth and kindness. She had not chosen to live a loveless life. That would be no one's first choice, if they had a say in the matter. Marta hadn't had a say in the matter, even as an adult, Earl thought, as he looked at her in the casket.

A good many people attended the funeral because in a farming town the size of this one just about everyone attends almost everybody else's baptism, wedding, and funeral. If one had not known the deceased personally, one would have known their spouse or child or brother or grandfather, and it would be un-neighborly not to pay one's respects. Melody turned to see who would want to attend her mother's funeral. She saw some families from the neighboring farms as well as the owner of the diner, whose name she did not know. Randy Larsen and Miss Wells were there; Jenny and the pharmacist were there, although Melody did not know who Jenny was. She imagined that some of the people she did not recognize had worked at the diner with her mother. Warren sat stiffly as he looked forward, his eyes unfocused.

Shortly before the service began, a woman whom Melody had never seen before entered the church. Melody was certain that she was part of her mother's family. She was a very pretty woman who looked a lot like her mother, but much younger, and without all the lines and creases that had crisscrossed her mother's face.

Melody leaned over and whispered to Warren, "Take a look at that woman over there standing by herself. Have you ever seen her before?"

Warren turned in his seat and took a good look at the woman. He said, "Not that I can remember, but I can't tell the difference between most grown-ups—they're just grown-ups."

"Don't you think she looks like *her*?"

"Yeah, I guess, but *she* wouldn't have gotten dressed up like that," Warren said.

"She looks enough like *her* that she could be her sister."

"She didn't have a sister."

"She never mentioned one," Melody said, "but I never believed anything she said. She had no pictures of anyone in her family and when I asked her about her family, she told me not to go nosing into other people's business."

The service began when the minister walked the three steps leading up to the right side of the altar and then across to the podium. He was a skinny man of about fifty with thinning brown hair and wire-rimmed glasses, wearing white vestments with a purple stole. The minister began by reading the passage from *The Book of Common Prayer* about earth to earth, ashes to ashes, dust to dust. He then looked up and let his gaze fall upon the congregation like a thin blanket unfurling as it is spread across a bed. He said that he had not had the privilege of knowing Marta, but that he had spoken with quite a number of people who knew her.

In somber tones, the minister began, "The person whose death we are here to mourn, Marta Bromfman, was a woman devoted to her family and to helping her neighbors. She worked tirelessly and thought of her own needs only after the needs of those around her had been met."

Warren and Melody did not recognize their mother in the words the pastor was speaking, and wondered if the other people in the church believed what they were hearing.

About a half hour into the service, the lulling monotone of the minister's voice was disrupted by the creaking of the door at the front of the church. The pastor paused momentarily to glance at the two people who were entering the church, which led the rest of the guests, with the exception of Warren, to turn and look. At first it was impossible to see who the two figures were because of the glare of white light streaming in from behind them. But after the smaller of the two figures twisted back to shut the door, and the two slowly made their way down the aisle, it became possible to discern that the couple was a white-haired old man and a small woman, much younger than he, probably his daughter. Bent forward, the man slowly walked down the center aisle, leaning alternately on the cane that he held in his right hand and on the woman whose shoulder was positioned under his left arm. Earl knew immediately who they were, and could not suppress his tears. This was the first time he'd wept since Marta died. The minister welcomed the two and waited until they were seated before continuing.

Despite Earl's protestations, his father and sister had done what they felt was right, and did so in a way that they hoped would cause Earl the least trouble. The afternoon before the funeral they boarded a Greyhound bus that took them west, across Tennessee and Missouri—a six-hour journey. They changed buses in the middle of the night in Kansas City, and again in Great Bend, before arriving at a bus terminal in town late in the morning. From there they took a taxi to the church that they both knew well.

Earl had seen Anne entering the church just before the service began. He had not seen her in fifteen years, but she looked exactly as he remembered her. She was thirty-three now but still had the glow of youth about her. She was wearing a black dress that was more formal and more stylish than the dresses any of the other women were wearing. But it was not this that set her apart. She was radiant. Earl saw in her the nineteen-year-old girl for whom music had been both the symptom and the cure. He pictured her in the attic apartment deciding which cuts to play for him from the collection of albums and singles she had brought.

Earl recalled the change in his life and Marta's that occurred in the days and weeks following the weekend in which Anne had brought her albums and record player. A rhythm of comings and goings took hold. Anne would arrive early Friday evening. Earl would have been in the apartment studying while Marta would have just returned from doing her book repair work at the library. They would go out for dinner when Anne arrived, talk and listen to music when they returned to the apartment, and go to sleep by 11:00—Earl and Marta in Earl's bedroom, Anne in Marta's. Earl and Marta put in a half-day's work at their jobs on Saturday mornings, looking forward to the afternoon as they had looked forward to recess in grade school. Anne would take the bus back to her apartment late Sunday afternoon. The tensions between Marta and Earl diminished to almost nothing since Earl no longer felt starved by Marta, and Marta no longer felt put upon by Earl. They asked very little of one another now that the anticipation of Anne's next visit was adding a future tense to their lives. Earl and Marta were becoming strangers to one another in the best sense of the word, which among other things, made them much more sexually exciting to one another. Without realizing it, they were seeing one another through Anne's eyes, and imagining Anne in one another. Sex, for both Earl and Marta, had been disappointing from the outset and had gone downhill from there. That summer, for the first time in her life, Marta learned what it was to experience lust, a feeling that she had never expected to feel and had never much wanted to feel. Earl knew what lust felt like, but had given up on ever feeling it with Marta. Earl's intense sexual desire for Anne had not diminished, but knowing that that desire would never be realized, he was able to enjoy the thought of sex with Anne while having sex with Marta. Marta had not overcome her feeling that Earl's ways were irritating, but she had come to feel that his ways were probably common to all men, and that he was probably the least irritating man she'd come across.

Earl was well liked among his football teammates and was able to borrow a car practically any time he wanted to. Marta and he, up to this point, had borrowed cars only to do errands in nearby towns. But going for a drive with Anne was nothing less than thrilling. Earl loved the feel of the warm summer air rushing in through the windows and the sound of the music from the car radio turned up loud. During these drives, he often thought, "It doesn't get better than this." As the summer proceeded, Earl became consumed with the feeling that time was running out. He had an ominous sense that there would be a return to life as he had lived it before Anne entered his life. But as is so often the case with life, he had been afraid of the wrong thing.

The autumn changes arrived as expected—the sharp bite of the morning air, the theft of light from the afternoon sky, the contortion of time as it is increasingly measured not by the rhythms of nature, but by the demands of work. All this was ordinary change, change within the limits of what was anticipated. But Marta, being unknowable, was unpredictable. In the evening of one of these autumn days, Marta asked Earl to sit and talk with her in the living room of their apartment—an unprecedented event. Once they were seated on the sofa about two feet apart, Marta straightened her skirt by pressing down on her thighs with the palms of both hands, pushing the material forward until she reached her knees.

She inhaled deeply before saying, "Earl, let me get right to the point. I've been keeping something from you for a few weeks. My period was late, which is not unusual, but as the weeks went by and nothing happened, I got worried. So I went to the University Health Center and they gave me a pregnancy test. They called me today and said the test was positive."

She paused for a response, but Earl was quiet.

"The doctor told me that I am six to eight weeks pregnant and that the baby is due around the beginning of May."

Earl searched Marta's face for a hint about how she was taking this, but he found none. Her face looked pale and angular as the light from the bare light bulb in the broken ceiling fixture made her forehead look shiny, while leaving dark shadows in the recesses of her eyes and cheeks and under her lower lip.

"Why have you waited all this time to tell me?" Earl asked, more accusingly than he had intended.

"My periods are irregular, and so I don't check in with you every time they're late."

Earl asked, "What do you want to do?"

"I definitely don't want to have an abortion. I've done some reading at the library. Abortion is illegal in every state, and I'm not going to let one of those illegal abortionists lay a hand on me."

"Please don't talk as if I want you to have an abortion," Earl said firmly. "We've talked about this many times when we were afraid you were pregnant and you know that I've never wanted you to get an abortion. I've wanted to marry you and raise the baby with you. I still want that and I hope that's what you want."

Even though Earl had turned on the couch toward Marta, she was slumped forward, her hands on her knees, looking at the floor.

"What I want I can't have," she said. Her voice was trembling. "I want *not* to be pregnant. I *don't* want to have a baby. But I *am* pregnant and I *am* going to have a baby. So the question is, what am I going to do with the baby? And my answer is, I'm *not* going to give it to a stranger. There are lots of things I *don't* want to do, and nothing I *do* want to do."

Earl said, "Please don't take from us the chance to make your having our baby a happy event in our lives."

"Happy event? Are you crazy? There's nothing happy about two college seniors who don't want to get married and don't want to have a baby finding out that they're going to have a baby and they can choose whether to go to a butcher and have it removed or to skip over their youth and jump right into middle age."

Earl, still trying to keep the conversation from becoming hysterical, said, "That's all true, but why not try to make the best we can of it? Why not say to ourselves that we love each other and that we're just speeding up what was going to happen by our own choice?"

Marta lifted her head slowly and looked over at Earl. "Do you believe a word you're saying? Love? You've never once told me that you love me and I've never once said it to you. Neither of us was expecting love. We like each other most of the time, we spend most of our time with each other, and we have sex once in a while. Is that love? I really don't know. Maybe it is."

"I wish you wouldn't denigrate what we have. I don't know what people mean when they talk about love. I've always figured that what anyone else means by love is their own business and it isn't going to be what I mean by it. There isn't a standard measure for love like Greenwich Mean Time. What I feel for you is a feeling I call love, and I don't want you squashing it like someone grinding a cigarette butt into the ground with their shoe."

Looking down at the floor again, Marta said, "Earl, I'm sorry."

Earl was surprised by Marta's apology. She had never apologized to him before about anything.

"I don't like the situation either," Earl said. "I wouldn't raise my hand if they asked, 'Who wants to give up what you were hoping to do when you graduate, forget about graduate school, and instead get married, raise a child, and work at the first job that comes along so you can pay the bills?' But nobody's asking me that. What they're asking is, 'What do you want to do with the baby you and Marta are going to have in May?' And I'm saying, 'I want to marry Marta and make a family with her.'"

Marta, still looking at the floor, said, "*We* had sex, but *I'm* pregnant. *I'm* going to have the baby, not you. I'm the mother. I don't agree with the women's lib goal of equal opportunity and equal responsibility for men and women. I believe that the mother is the only one who really loves the children. Men might go through the motions, but I don't believe that they really care in the same way that women do. It's biological. Women have breasts to feed babies, men don't. You'll get a job, and I know that you'll do well at it and be appreciated for it. And you'll come home and ask me how my day with the baby has been, and my answer will be of less interest to you than what you hear on the evening news. You'll notice if there's no dinner on the table and no food in the refrigerator, but that's not going to happen because I'm not the kind of person who lets that happen. I will do the shopping and the cooking and cleaning. I'll change the baby's diapers and take the baby out in a stroller to get some air. You'll have to get a job to pay the bills. I won't even have that option, not because you won't give it to me, but because I wouldn't trust you or any other man to take care of a baby. You could fake it—and you're the type that would try—but you couldn't really do it. I wouldn't do that to a baby."

"There's nothing I can say that makes any difference to you. You have your mind made up that this is going to be a disaster that will end your life, but not mine. I can't make a logical argument to counter each of your claims. All I can do is hope that you can feel that I genuinely want to make a family with you and I don't believe that having this baby will mean that our lives are over … or that yours is over, and mine isn't."

Earl had been leaning forward on the couch in a failed effort to catch Marta's eyes with his. When he finished speaking he leaned back on the couch. Marta remained hunched over.

Finally, she said, "Earl, I know that you believe what you're saying, I really do, and I would love to believe it too. But because it's so different from what my gut tells me is going to happen, it feels like we're even farther apart than I thought we'd be. You seem naïve to me. I've always liked that about you, even when your naïveté makes me furious at you for not seeing the world for what it is."

Earl, too, was frightened that Marta's version of what was in store for them was more accurate than his, but he didn't think that there was any point in giving in to those fears. He knew that he did not love Marta in the way that he had hoped one day to love the woman he'd marry and with whom he'd have children. He also knew that Marta did not love him in the way he had hoped his wife would love him. During the two years he had been living with Marta, he had many times asked himself what he was doing there with a woman he both liked and pitied, but did not love. He would say to himself that neither of them had promised anything to the other, and that on graduating, they would end up in different graduate schools or accept jobs in different cities, and that would be the end of their relationship. Earl's degree was in engineering and he hoped to work for a company like General Electric or Westinghouse, a large company that had branches all over the country and all over the world. He planned to make his applications to these and other engineering companies in the spring semester. Marta was enamored with book restoration and repair, and had planned to get a graduate degree in library sciences. The book restoration department had already offered to help her pay for graduate school so she could one day return and work in the rare books section of the library. Earl knew that all of those hopes, both his and Marta's, were now in great jeopardy, if not extinguished completely. Their lives after graduation would not be what they had planned. How good or bad things would be for them was to a large extent up to the two of them, Earl thought. He knew that he had to be the one to keep alive their dreams, even though those dreams had not included one another. If he didn't do it, no one would.

During the next weeks, Earl and Marta gradually absorbed the shock of the news. They had to reinvent themselves in their own minds. No longer were they college kids. They were only months away from being the parents of an infant. This change in self-definition was even more wrenching for Marta than it was for Earl because Marta had great difficulty imagining herself as a mother and as a wife. It was only in the course of these weeks of self-reflection that Marta put into words for herself the fact that she had not planned ever to marry or have children. She thought that she did not have in her either the wish or the ability to be a wife or a mother. What came as a surprise to her was that she was emotionally incapable of giving her child up for adoption. Where, she wondered, did that come from? Certainly not from either of her parents who, she believed, hated the burden of having children and found absolutely no pleasure in it. She didn't think that she had been a particularly good older sister to Anne. She had jumped ship her senior year of high school without giving Anne a second thought.

There was very little time in which to make these decisions if there was to be any hope of hiding the fact that the baby had been conceived before they were married, a fact that, for Marta, was very important to keep secret. She did not want her child to live in shame as she did. In the end, Marta made up her mind to marry Earl and have the baby. Earl never betrayed to anyone his fears and disappointments about making a family with Marta.

Earl Bromfman and Marta Noel were married at the county seat on October 29, 1964. Anne Noel's signature appears on the marriage license as witness to the event.

In the late afternoon of the day of their marriage, Earl telephoned his parents to tell them that he and Marta had gotten married in a civil ceremony that day, and that he wanted them to be the first to know. He explained that he and Marta had not wanted to make a big deal of it—it just wasn't their style. Fortunately, Marta had finally consented to meet Earl's parents over the spring break earlier in the year, so Earl was not now in the position of telling them that he had married someone whom they had never met. His parents were startled at first by the announcement of the wedding, but then seemed genuinely happy for him and told him how much they liked Marta and how eager they were to meet her family. They asked Earl to put Marta on the phone so they could congratulate her and welcome her to the family. Earl then called his brother and sister.

Marta did not call anyone.

EIGHT

Toward the end of the fall semester of her senior year, six weeks after marrying Earl, Marta found a letter from the comptroller's office of the university in her mail box. This was not unexpected because at the end of each of the previous semesters she had received letters from the comptroller's office confirming the extension of her work-study scholarship. But before opening the envelope, Marta had a premonition that this letter was different from the others. She put the unopened envelope into the pocket of her green loden coat, and made her way up the four flights of stairs to the top floor. The apartment was dark, lit only on one side by the trapezoids of light on the ceiling cast by the streetlights in front of the building and the headlights of the occasional passing car. Marta let her backpack drop to the floor and made her way to her bedroom. She turned on the desk lamp and removed the letter from her coat pocket. With her heart pounding, she clumsily tore open the envelope.

Dear Miss Noel,

We are writing to inform you that an audit has raised some questions about your application for the University Work-Study Program. Would you kindly make an appointment

with one of us in the Comptroller's Office to clear up this
matter.

Sincerely,
Francine Gallagher
Assistant Comptroller

As Marta read the letter, a chill went through her. For almost four years, she had been pushing to the back of her mind the fear of being arrested for forgery. In her initial application for financial aid she had made up figures for her parents' income and forged her father's signature. Marta had expected that after her initial financial aid request had been processed and approved, she would never have to face that piece of deception again. But at the end of the first semester of her freshman year, she received a form from the comptroller's office that asked for her father's signature attesting to the fact that his financial situation had not changed during the period since the initial application was submitted. At the time that Marta first forged her father's signature, she did not have a sample of the signature to use as a template for her forgery, so all she could do was to create a signature that did not look like her own. She had been so anxious about engaging in forgery that she neglected to make a copy of the initial application with the forged signature on it. Consequently, when she received the notice from the comptroller's office at the end of her first semester asking for confirmation that her father's income hadn't changed, she made a second forgery of his signature and hoped that it looked like the first. She kept a copy of the second forgery, which she used as the model for the forgeries on the subsequent semi-annual requests for updates from the comptroller's office.

On reading the letter, Marta, still wearing her winter coat, collapsed into her desk chair trying to pull herself out of the whirlpool of horrifying images of being arrested, tried, and found guilty of forgery. Her image of her father's face, contorted with disdain and contempt, grew larger and larger, his

112

mouth open, exposing his foul yellow teeth. The stench of his breath was nauseating. She retched into the metal wastebasket, which she grabbed from under her desk. After slowly, deliberately wiping the sides of her mouth with tissues that she took from her pocketbook, she made her way unsteadily to the bed, using the edge of the bed to support herself. As she lay on her bed staring at the ceiling, it did not occur to Marta to talk to Earl about this—she was alone to fend for herself, as she always had been. Unable to devise a strategy, and wanting to get this "matter" over with, whatever the outcome, she stumbled down the dark hallway of the apartment to the telephone on the kitchen wall and arranged an appointment with Miss Gallagher at 3:45 the following day.

When Earl returned to the apartment a couple of hours later, Marta's backpack was on the floor next to the front door. The door to her room was shut, with no light visible under the door. He assumed she was asleep and did not disturb her. She lay on her bed all night, her mind flooded with terrifying images, not knowing whether she was awake or dreaming. She watched the December dawn throw filthy gray light through her windows into her room.

Marta dressed, put on her winter coat and made her way down the stairs and out the front door of the building. The cold mist washed over her face. Marta walked across the campus, down the hill into the run-down business district of the town, and found herself in the railway yard. Hulking boxcars, flats, and tank cars stood still as if they were enormous animals frozen in place, one hooked to the next by blackened couplers, each ensuring the captivity of the next. The sharp sound of metallic clanking mingled with the soft murmurings of men's voices wafted over the skein of frigid tracks.

Hours passed unnoticed. Marta's dread of the meeting with the assistant to the comptroller was never for a second out of mind, though the shape of its presence changed continually, at one moment taking the form of a dull ache in Marta's chest;

the next moment taking the shape of an aerial view of herself in which she watched herself become smaller and smaller as the point of observation moved farther and farther from the surface of the earth, finally reaching a vantage point from which she was invisible—indistinguishable from everything else; and at still other moments, the dread took the shape of a vivid image of herself floating endlessly into empty space, feeling herself drifting into absolute darkness.

The sound of the ringing of the bell in Whitman Tower in the South Quad of the campus seemed to Marta to be a signal demanding that she return to the apartment, where she bathed, put on a crisp white cotton blouse, a plaid skirt, and a teal blue cardigan. She looked in the full-length mirror on the back of the door to her room and saw her mother.

Marta allowed more than two hours to get to the comptroller's office because she did not trust her sense of time. She checked to see whether the time on her watch coincided with that of the clock in the kitchen. As she walked down the front steps of her building, the campus paths were packed with students as well as some other people who struck her as odd—a man walking on crutches who seemed not to need them, three boys who looked too young to be college students, a professor carrying a briefcase who seemed somehow too dignified, too important for this campus of the university.

As the time approached 3:00, she checked her watch every minute or so. Marta decided to walk around the building in which the comptroller's office was located until five minutes before her 3:45 appointment. The building used to be the physics building before a new complex was built for the physics department, which was equipped with the latest cyclotron or some other piece of equipment the name of which Marta could not remember. She could see carved into the stone above the doorway to the building the name "Converse Hall Department of Physics" over which black letters of the same size were bolted, which read "Merrill Administrative Center." The carved letters seemed to be rebelling against the newer and louder overlaid letters, which were trying unsuccessfully to pretend the carved letters did not exist.

At 3:40, Marta walked into the comptroller's office, a room much larger than she had expected. What kind of word was "comptroller?" Are there any other words in the English language in which the letters "mp" are pronounced as if they were an "n"? The office looked like a bank without tellers' windows. There was a long counter extending the length of the rectangular room with two middle-aged women standing behind it methodically thumbing through stacks of paper as if there was something very specific they were trying to find. The room was lit by two rows of six-foot-long, white fluorescent light fixtures spaced five or six feet apart, as if they were a pair of rows of science fiction tanks ready for orders to move forward. Ten feet or so behind the long counter were a half-dozen dark oak desks, each with an IBM Selectric typewriter neatly centered in front of the desk chair, a table lamp with a green glass shade on the right hand corner of the desk, and a three-tiered in-and-out-basket at the far left corner. Nothing was left to chance, Marta thought. Behind two of the desks were two women with wire-rimmed glasses, their hair pulled back in buns, their faces stark, without a bit of make-up. They looked eerily like one another, as if they were clones. Marta didn't know if one of these women was Miss Gallagher.

Having determined that the younger of the two women at the counter looked less menacing than the other, Marta walked up to her and told the woman her name. Receiving a blank stare in return, she told the woman the name of the person whom she was there to see, and the appointment time. Marta was told to take a seat. She turned and noticed for the first time the three long, highly polished, backless benches opposite the counter. She suspected that this dance was being choreographed in a way that would maximize her feelings of weakness and fear.

But it wasn't working on her. She had been through far worse than these women could dish out.

After about fifteen minutes, she was told to go to Miss Gallagher's desk, which was the one farthest to the left. Miss Gallagher, seemingly absorbed in important work, remained seated, her eyes fixed on the piece of paper she was reading as Marta approached. After making Marta stand awkwardly by the side of the desk for a long few seconds, Miss Gallagher looked up and said, "Miss Noel," and with a nod of her head motioned Marta to sit in the straight-backed, wooden chair across the desk from her.

"Miss Noel, I see here ..."

"It's Mrs. Bromfman. I married in October."

"I see. So, Mrs. Bromfman, as you were told in the letter you received from this office, some puzzling things have come to our attention during a review of the records of students in the work-study program. Your initial application and the six subsequent requests for continuation of that financial aid package were signed by Lawrence Noel. It says here he's your father. Is that correct?"

"Yes, it is."

"It came to the attention of one of the auditors that your father's original signature looked nothing like the signatures on the seven subsequent requests for continued aid. Can you explain that?"

"I don't know how to explain it."

"Did he have a stroke?"

"No, I don't think so. I don't see him very often."

"Did your father sign these documents?"

"I assume he did if his signature is on them."

"Mrs. Bromfman, I urge you to be fully forthcoming. Anything less than the truth will make matters very difficult."

Marta looked into Miss Gallagher's piercing blue eyes trying to find a hint of kindness, but found none. Marta realized at that moment that she, at her best, was an amateur, a mere child,

116

playing against a master at this game. Miss Gallagher was not the sort who helps people find solutions; she was a prosecutor who proved people guilty of a crime. And Marta knew full well she was not at her best, she was not even a skilled amateur in her current state. Marta decided to tell the truth because she felt incapable of keeping straight a series of lies. Whatever was going to happen would happen, and she felt absolutely powerless to alter what was in store for her.

Marta said in a thin, monotone voice, "I'm ashamed of myself and I'm ashamed of my parents. By the time I was going into my junior year of high school things were so bad at home that I had to move out. The school principal, Miss Saunders, thought I had unusual potential, right from my freshman year, and she was generous enough to be a mentor for me. When it became clear that I couldn't live at home any longer, she said I could take a room in her house until I graduated. My parents were angry about my moving out, but they didn't make a complaint to the police or the school or even to Miss Saunders. I don't think they wanted anyone to ask questions about the situation. They're not ordinary parents, they're different."

Marta had decided to tell the truth, but she was stunned by the fact that she was telling this woman, whom she neither liked nor trusted, more of the truth than she had told anyone else in her life, except Earl.

Miss Gallagher's eyes were glued to Marta's, trying to discern what was fact and what was manipulation.

She said, after a pause that felt to Marta as if it were several minutes long, "Parents sometimes have a hard time with a child and removing the child from the home is the only option. These things happen in families. But we're not here for a discussion of the problems you had with your parents or they had with you, we're here to get to the bottom of the change in your father's signature."

"I'm trying to tell you the circumstances in which I signed the form with my father's signature," Marta said. "When I asked him to supply the information needed to complete the financial aid application and to sign it, he refused. He told me that my wanting to go to college was just another example of my having a swelled head and that I should go to secretarial school. I didn't want to be a secretary. He was angry about my moving out and wanted to get back at me. I signed his name because that was the only way I could manage to pay the tuition and all the other expenses."

As the word "secretary" came out of Marta's mouth, she worried that she had made a terrible blunder. Did Miss Gallagher consider herself a secretary? Was an "assistant comptroller" an executive position or a secretarial one?

Miss Gallagher looked incredulous.

"Did it ever occur to you to work for a year or two to save up the money you needed instead of engaging in forgery and misrepresentation to the state? Those are serious crimes. People go to prison for forgery and fraud."

Marta asked, "Do I need a lawyer?"

"That's entirely up to you. I can't advise you on that. To your credit you have been honest about what we suspected to be the case, which we confirmed by talking with your father."

Marta realized that Miss Gallagher had known the whole story from the beginning and had taken pleasure in waiting to see if she would try to add further lies to her previous deceptions. But even worse, Miss Gallagher somehow knew that the most terrible punishment she could inflict was not turning Marta over to the dean of students for expulsion or even reporting her to the police for forgery and fraud. Far more terrifying to Marta was the rage she imagined her father letting loose upon her for lying and stealing and dragging him and the whole family into the gutter along with her. The fact she had not seen or spoken to her father for years did not diminish in the least the terror she felt.

But Miss Gallagher had not yet played her final trump card.

"We are also taking a very dim view of the role that your father tells us Miss Saunders played in your repeated deceptions. Is it true, as he has told us, that Miss Saunders assisted you in the preparation of the application and in the forgery scheme?"

"No, that is not true," Marta protested, raising her voice for the first time. "That's a lie, and I think that you know that it's a lie. She helped me get the applications for admission to the university and the work-study program, but she knew nothing about my making up the figures concerning my father's income and knew nothing about the fact that I signed his signature on the financial aid forms. The reason I think that you know that the accusation against Miss Saunders is groundless is that you know that if she had been in on it, she would have known to keep the original forgery so I would have it in case I had to use it again."

Marta no longer felt in control of the connection between her thoughts and the words she spoke. Words came from her mouth, but she did not know ahead of time what they would be, and she did not know what she had already said. She heard herself saying—how loudly she could not be sure—"Miss Saunders is the only person in my life who has ever cared what happened to me."

Miss Gallagher, unmoved by Marta's defense of Miss Saunders, said, "Certainly we don't take anybody's word for what Miss Saunders may or may not have known or done until we speak with her, but I should tell you that your father indicated that he was going to report her to the school superintendant."

Marta's voice trembled as she said, "Don't pretend that you're not trying to destroy Miss Saunders. Could it be that you know that she's a better person than you are, and that there's more satisfaction in life to be had from helping students than by persecuting them? Is that why you're assisting my father in bringing her down? You don't have to answer me, there will be plenty of time to ask yourself that question."

"I think that lying and finger-pointing come far too easily to you, Mrs. Bromfman. *Your* behavior is the only reason why we're talking about Miss Saunders. If anyone's responsible for 'bringing her down,' as you so melodramatically put it, it's you."

This last attack by Miss Gallagher was a knock-out blow to an already reeling boxer. Marta sat in her chair ashen-faced and speechless. She could see Miss Gallagher's lips moving, but she could no longer hear what she was saying. Eventually, Miss Gallagher stood up from behind her desk, which Marta took as a sign that she should leave. Marta stood and looked around the room for the door to the office through which she had entered and through which she should now leave. But the room was spinning and the noise in her head was deafening.

She could hear Miss Gallagher saying with raised voice, "Mrs. Bromfman, we're finished for today. You should leave now."

The woman behind the counter whom Marta had spoken with earlier heard the commotion and walked briskly to where Marta was standing, took her gently by the elbow, and walked her to the bench on which she had sat earlier.

The woman sat next to Marta and said, "I'll sit here with you until you feel stronger."

Marta looked at her blankly. After some period of time, Marta got to her feet and made her way out of the comptroller's office, down the stairs and into the cold, dark air. The lights above the paths were on, so it must have been after 5:00. Marta was empty of thoughts. She walked back to the building where she lived, climbed the four flights of stairs to the apartment, and unlocked the front door, but afterwards had no memory of anything that had occurred after she watched Miss Gallagher's lips moving without any comprehensible words coming from her mouth.

NINE

A fter the last amen was said in the funeral service, the guests slowly stood and waited quietly for a clearing in the movement of bodies down the center aisle. Earl, Melody, and Warren, in the front row, remained seated, staring ahead of them at the deserted altar. The guests, on stepping over the threshold of the front door of the church, were lashed by the white-hot rays of the noonday sun. Many held their palms to their foreheads as a makeshift visor, while others stooped, eyes to the ground, as they made their way forward, as if ducking under the blades of a helicopter.

As the guests rounded the southwest corner of the building, they found themselves in the dark shadow cast by the nave of the church. They paused as their eyes adapted to the dimmer light. Earl, Warren, and Melody were led by the minister through a side door in back of the altar. The four of them walked the length of the church to a spot in the shade where Earl and his children stood in a row accepting the condolences and good wishes of the guests, some shaking hands, some hugging, and others giving kisses on the cheek to the grieving family.

Melody was wearing the dark blue dress and black satin shoes that Miss Wells had given her as a gift, asking nothing in return, but clearly taking great pleasure in being able to do this for Melody. The kindness that Miss Wells had shown Melody was still alive in her as she stood between Earl and Warren accepting the sympathy of the guests who were filing by. Melody was feeling something—a set of things really—that she hadn't before. While she didn't have words that fully described it, she had never felt prettier and better loved. And of all times and of all places, she was feeling this as she stood with her father and brother at her mother's funeral.

Groups of mourners stood in the shade of the towering oaks and maples on the west side of the church, but the thick, warm air made it difficult to breathe, particularly for the older guests, who quickly sought chairs to rest on. The members of the Women's Church Auxiliary had set up three long, portable tables with white tablecloths on which they had placed evenly spaced pitchers of iced tea with sliced lemon among pine sprigs and wild flowers. They had also prepared large bowls of fruit gelatin, sherbet punch, and other refreshments that their husbands carried rapidly from their cars and pickup trucks and placed on the tables precisely where the wives specified. Despite every effort, the gelatin and sherbet were half melted by the time they arrived at their designated spot. They looked like leftovers from the previous day.

The owner of the diner where Marta had worked, along with the waitresses, cooks, and dishwashers, brought platters of sandwiches and cakes that they had prepared the previous day and early that morning. Earl thanked the owner and offered to pay for the food, but he would have none of it. He said that he had liked Marta very much and that she had never once let him down in all the years he'd known her.

Earl carried three folding chairs to the pavement next to the side of the church where he helped his father lower himself into one of the seats. Henry felt light in Earl's hands—his short-sleeved white shirt clinging to his sweat-drenched chest and back, his belt pulled to its last notch bunching the fabric of his pants in front. Earl unfolded two other chairs for himself and Leslie, which he placed on either side of his father's. It had been two years since Earl's mother's funeral in North Carolina, which was the last time Earl had seen his father and sister. Time seemed not to have touched Leslie as much as it had Earl and his father. Leslie was not a beauty, but she was an extraordinarily generous soul and had a type of intelligence and wit that conveyed such compassion and understanding that her lack of beauty was inconsequential to her attractiveness as a woman. She had never lacked for boys eager to take her to school and church events. Leslie married Ron Adler, a journalist whom she met when she was in college and he was a young reporter for the local newspaper. Earl had been impressed from the time he was a boy by the way in which his little sister was able to find something surprising and interesting in what seemed mundane to him. She found characters and stories in the clustering of stars in the night, ignoring the tired constellations listed in the almanac, finding her own serpents and heroes and princesses.

Earl remembered Leslie reading him the opening pages of *Of Mice and Men*, which was the first time Earl genuinely came to know that books were not simply pages to get through in order to complete homework assignments. Sitting by the church with Leslie and their father, he recalled vividly the intensity of the feelings he'd had—feelings he couldn't name—while listening to Leslie read *Of Mice and Men* to him. He remembered that he'd been choked with tears and had had to make a concerted effort not to let his voice crack when he spoke to Leslie when she finished reading. He had managed to say that what she'd read was beautiful, but it wasn't just beautiful. And, in response, Leslie had said that it wasn't just beautiful, it was ominous because you knew right from the beginning that something terrible was going to happen—something awful and unfair and wrong. All these years later, he remembered her saying that, and how astounded he was that she'd been able to put words to what he'd been feeling.

And now too, as he listened to Leslie talk, he heard in the sound of her voice so much of who she was. From the time she was very young, she was such an unlikely mixture of innocence and uncanny intelligence. As her older brother, Earl had not only been proud of her, he'd been in awe of her. Now, as he watched her talking, he saw his mother in her, his mother as a woman with a second chance at life, a life in which circumstances allowed her time and place to use her mind in more interesting ways than those available to a small-town farmer's wife with a high school education.

Leslie must have been only thirteen or fourteen when she read to him—not just *Of Mice and Men*, but other books she thought he'd like. How odd it was, he thought, for a sixteen-year-old boy to be read to by his twelve-year-old sister. Without saying a word, they'd go to their bedroom and Leslie would read to him. His favorite book was *The Heart is a Lonely Hunter*, maybe because it was Leslie's favorite too. The rest of the family made no mention of Leslie's reading to Earl—such a simple act of kindness on all their parts—so as not to embarrass him.

Leslie said to Earl, "I'm so sorry about Marta's death. I never got to know her very well."

Earl replied, "I'm not sure anyone did. She was a very private person."

"Your mother got to know her as much as anyone in the family did," Henry said, struggling to get the words out because the heat of the day was causing him to have trouble catching his breath. "She told me many times that she wished she could do something to lift the worry from her. But that was your mother. She wanted to help everyone who was suffering. She was never a martyr. She just couldn't imagine not doing what she did for people. I was thinking how she'd have wanted to be here today to help you and the children."

"Even Mom would have found it hard to help Marta," Earl said as he looked out at the field of parched grass behind the church. "Marta had trouble accepting anything from anyone. I tried. The children tried. I shouldn't be talking about Marta this way at her funeral. She didn't ask anything of anyone that she didn't ask of herself."

Leslie never said anything she didn't mean, though she was considerate in what she said. She couldn't stand exchanging empty pleasantries, not because such talk was fake or dishonest, but because it was terribly boring. She had always liked Earl's honesty.

She said to Earl, "Marta always seemed lonely to me. I felt bad for her. But Earl, it couldn't have been easy for you either."

"No, specially in the last year or so. Something happened. Maybe it was just the fact of getting older. She became embittered in a way that seemed to consume her. Nothing had worked out as she had hoped."

Henry said, "Melody and Warren have such good hearts. She must have done something right in raising them. Look at them over there talking together. Melody is so beautiful and lady-like, and Warren is a fine boy. She had to be proud of them."

Earl's eyes met Leslie's as they silently agreed not to disabuse their father of his illusions.

Earl was well aware that Leslie, out of respect for his privacy, was not asking him about the most sensitive matters, not asking the most painful questions, questions that no one dared ask, except for Randy Larsen. What had led to up to that fateful morning? What exactly had Marta done to force Earl to kill her? Why couldn't he have used less force in stopping her? And most unspeakable of all, had Earl intended to kill her?

As they talked, Earl felt grateful to his father and Leslie for having traveled such a long way to be with him and Warren and Melody. He had not anticipated how much difference it would make to have them there, how much it still meant to him to be part of his childhood family. Their presence was important to Melody and Warren too. Despite the fact that they had not seen their grandfather and aunt in a long time, they spoke to them on the phone quite often and exchanged occasional letters. But their favorite member of their father's family had been their Gramma Flora. They not only loved her, they admired her and were proud of her. She would say things, as if to herself, such as, "Raising one's voice never helped anybody hear any better," and "People are sure they're right just because they're saying it," and "He's talking as if God whispered it in his ear." If anyone were to ask her about what she had said under her breath, she would reply, "Don't pay any attention to me. I'm just an old woman talking to herself," and then she'd give a surreptitious wink to Warren and Melody, her co-conspirators. They thought that the things their grandmother said were the smartest things anybody in the family said, even their father. At night in their room, they would repeat her words in a voice that sounded like hers, and then laugh—sometimes so hard they couldn't stop—because her way of putting things was just right, just what they were feeling.

Earl was so involved with his family that he was oblivious to the presence of Randy Larsen. Randy was struck by the well-dressed woman who bore a striking resemblance to Marta, and yet looked far more worldly than Marta—or anybody else he had ever met, for that matter. To say that Randy had been watching her from the moment that she made her late, and somewhat dramatic, entry into the church would be a gross understatement. He was mesmerized by her. She wore a tailored black sleeveless dress over which a thin black shawl seemed to float. His eyes were drawn to the vertical slit—only six inches or so—at the hemline of the back of the dress, which made the dress very sexy. Also eye-catching for Randy, was an inch or so of barely visible black lace sewn along the contour of the neckline. To put it simply, she was one of the most beautiful women he had ever seen. But despite his lengthy scrutiny, he could not get a read on her. Had she been airlifted in from another world? Were the people of this simple farming community a curiosity to her, much as she was to them? Or was she coming home, returning to something that was all too familiar to her, something she had tried to escape, but kept pulling her back?

She held a glass of iced tea in her right hand as she moved unobtrusively from one spot to another, not letting her eyes meet those of anyone else. Randy finally decided to introduce himself to her. He felt as he had when he first asked a girl to dance at a church party. He told her that he was a long-time friend of Earl's and knew Marta only casually. Casual was an odd word, he thought, to describe anything related to Marta. He said that even though he had never seen her before, she looked so much like Marta that he thought she might be her sister.

Anne looked him in the eye questioningly as he spoke, which he found disconcerting.

She said, "Yes, I am Marta's younger sister."

After a few rounds of awkward small talk about his having played football with Earl and the unusually hot weather, Randy said, "I'm a deputy sheriff around here, and I may not have a chance to talk with you before you leave, so I'd like to get your help with a few details about your sister."

Anne replied coolly, "I'm stunned that you would choose Marta's funeral as the place to do your police work. I'd suggest that you find a more appropriate time and place to make your inquiries."

Randy, now red-faced, said, "I owe you an apology."

Anne did not walk away from him; she looked at him in such disbelief that he turned and left.

Melody saw Deputy Larsen talking with the woman who looked like her mother, which made Melody all the more curious about her. She took her father aside and asked him who that woman was.

"She's your mother's younger sister, Anne. I know you'll have lots of questions, but they'll have to wait."

"Wait for what?"

"Till later."

"How much later?"

"Melody," Earl said with uncharacteristic firmness, "there are things that are so complicated that they have to find their own time to be told."

Earl's thoughts and musings had taken on a life of their own since Marta's death. His thoughts seemed to go where they wanted to and took him with them. After the brief exchange with Melody about Anne, his thoughts drew him back to that terrible autumn at the university. Images and words and sounds and bodily sensations crowded in on him. They were all part of a single undefinable thing, and that "thing" lay at the core of who Earl was then, and now. It felt to Earl that he did not have memories of that period of his life; it was more that he had holes in him through which he was pulled back into those days with such force that it was pointless to fight it.

One image haunted him more than any other: the sight of Marta entering the apartment on that dark afternoon in December. Her face was without expression, all the muscles seemingly having been released from connection with the contents of her mind. She walked, but her gait was not her gait, not even her gait when she was exhausted or terribly discouraged or furious at him and the rest of the world. He knew the moment he saw her that Marta was no longer herself, not in the sense of feeling out of sorts, but in the sense of having died.

Earl approached her calmly, so as not to frighten her, and then used all of his strength to keep her from collapsing to the floor. He lifted her right arm and tried to wrap it around his shoulder and neck. She weakly pushed him away, but he ignored that. Earl walked her to her room as gently as he could. Having sat her down on the side of her bed, he removed her coat and boots and laid her down on the top of her bed, with her head on her pillow. The room was lit only by the gray-black residue of daylight coming through the window, which settled on everything it touched like a thin dusting of soot. Earl took off his shoes and lay down on his back beside her, his arm barely touching hers. They lay there for a time drifting in and out of sleep. The room became black, lit only by the irregular shapes the streetlights cast on the ceiling.

Some time during the next few hours, Earl said softly, "Marta, I know that something terrible has happened, the worst thing that has ever happened to you. I don't know what it is, and I don't have to know what it is to know that it is horrific."

Marta's body was rigid and motionless next to his. They lay there in silence, for how long, Earl did not know. It did not matter. The feeling of their arms touching was utterly impersonal.

Some time in the middle of the night, Earl realized that the room was very cold. Like a blind man, he felt his way to the closet, pulled out two blankets from the upper shelf and spread them over Marta. He picked up Marta's boots, put them in her closet and then hung her coat on the coat rack in the hall, almost as if he were a nurse tidying up the hospital room of a dying patient as she slept a sleep that would not be restorative for her. Earl crawled under the blankets slowly and carefully in order not to disturb Marta.

As the night wore on, the ache of emptiness in Earl's chest grew increasingly painful. He awoke periodically feeling the ache, and for a moment did not remember why he was feeling it.

Earl had been awake for quite a while watching the light from the window turn from sallow yellow to milky white when Marta awoke with a start. She wrestled with the blankets as if they were intentionally holding her down. Once on her feet, she stared at Earl who was still half under the blankets, fully clothed on the opposite side of the bed. Marta's face was pale and her eyes sunken.

She snapped at Earl, "What are you doing in my room?"

"You were in a daze when you got home yesterday. I've never seen you that way before."

Marta interrupted saying, "I don't believe a word you're saying. You don't fool me. I know who you're not."

"Who I'm not?"

Even though he looked like Earl and was talking like Earl, Marta knew he was not Earl. Had Earl all along been someone other than the person he appeared to be? He had always had a way of smooth-talking her. Whoever this man in her room was, he was trying to sell her the story that it was she who had changed, and that was why she did not recognize him.

"I'm your husband, you know that," Earl said.

"No, I don't know that. What do you want?"

"Marta …"

Interrupting him, she yelled, "I'm not fooled by you."

Earl said, "Please calm down so we can talk this out."

"You can talk all you want, but I'm on to you."

"Just let me say two or three sentences. Then I'll stop and you can decide if you want to hear more."

Marta's heart was pounding violently. She didn't know whether this man was working alone or whether he was in this with other people.

Earl took the absence of a refusal as permission to talk.

"Late yesterday afternoon, when you got home, you were in a state of shock. I don't know what happened to you, but it was something awful. You didn't seem to know where you were. I thought that you needed rest so I helped you get into bed. I was worried about you so I lay next to you. That's all."

Marta had stopped listening to this man after he spoke his first few words. Her mind was on how to get free of him. Things were moving so fast she could not make a plan. She looked around the room, her head turning quickly in one direction and then the next.

"I'm getting out of here. What have you done with my things?"

130

"I put your boots in your closet and hung your coat on the hooks opposite the front door."

Marta saw a closet door. The door was ajar. She was frightened by what might be in it.

"You get the boots out of there."

It was clear to Earl that nothing was familiar to Marta and everything felt dangerous to her. He was out of his depth in trying to deal with her. Earl opened the closet door and retrieved Marta's boots. She sat on the side of the bed, but was so distracted that she had a great deal of trouble getting her boots on. It was as if she couldn't get her mind and her hands to work together. After she finally squeezed her feet into the boots, Marta left the room. Earl could hear her put on her coat, open the front door, and cautiously begin to descend the stairs.

The stairway felt vaguely familiar to Marta, and at the same time, everything was new and foreboding. At each landing she expected to be stopped by a man waiting for her. After finally reaching the bank of mailboxes on the ground floor, she was terrified that the front door to the building would be locked. It wasn't. But as she pulled it open, she was blinded by the glare of the sun coming through the glass storm door. As if hit in the face, she lurched backwards, unable to see anything but flashing dots of colored light. She groped her way to a wall and leaned her body against it. Gradually she recovered her sight. This time she carefully approached the front door. Directing her eyes to the ground and holding her right hand outstretched in front of her, she moved slowly toward the door until her hand was met by glass. With her eyes still cast downward, she realized that the glass was the glass of an aluminum storm door, which she opened. The cold wind bit her face, but she was familiar with air of this type. It did not distract her from the task of making her escape. On the stoop, Marta slowly lifted her gaze and saw a street running in front of the building, and across the street, she saw a tangle of plowed pathways, with snow piled high on both sides of each path. Marta could vaguely make out buildings beyond the leafless branches of trees.

She cautiously crossed the street and decided to turn left on the path that ran parallel to the street. She had no way of knowing if this was the safest of the paths. Marta was startled by the loud hiss made by a car speeding past her on the shiny black surface of the wet street. The air was full of menacing noise. The sound of her boots crushing the snow beneath them was as loud as firecrackers. The trees rattled as if trying to talk as the wind knocked the bare branches against one another. A man wearing a long toffee-colored coat suddenly appeared on the opposite side of the street walking in the same direction she was headed. He was walking at exactly the same pace as she was, stride for stride. He looked across at her through the space between his dark gray stocking cap pulled down across his forehead and the maroon scarf that covered his nose and mouth. Marta spun around and walked rapidly in the direction from which she had come. She could not get the image of the man's eyes out of her mind. By the time she gathered herself sufficiently to look around, he was gone and she was lost. She did not know if she had passed the building she had come from. She stood paralyzed with fear.

Earl had been watching Marta from the kitchen window of the apartment. He saw her turn to walk back in the direction of the apartment. She did not have a key to the front door so he went down to the entryway to unlock it, but found that it had been left open. He pretended to be getting his mail from the bank of mailboxes near the front door. After a minute or two of waiting, Earl walked out onto the front stoop. He saw Marta standing across the street, about a hundred yards to his right. Earl sensed that she was lost, but decided not to go after her, and instead to let her come to him. Dazed, Marta walked toward Earl. When she finally reached him, she walked past him into the ground floor hallway, up the four flights of stairs, through the open door to the apartment, and into her room, closing and locking the door behind her.

With Marta back in her room, Earl called the University Health Center from the kitchen phone and asked to speak to the on-call psychiatrist. The woman who answered the phone asked Earl to give her his phone number so the doctor could call him back. Ten minutes later, the phone rang. The psychiatrist introduced himself as Dr. Hensley, and asked Earl about the nature of his relationship with the woman whose behavior alarmed him. Earl told him that they had been married for six weeks. Dr. Hensley asked Earl to describe his wife's behavior. Earl spoke softly, not wanting Marta to hear what he was saying. The psychiatrist told Earl to bring Marta to the health center, where he would meet them in half an hour. Earl said that he was certain that Marta would refuse to see a doctor or to go anywhere with him. Dr. Hensley seemed annoyed by this. Earl added that he would like to do everything possible to avoid a physical struggle because Marta was pregnant.

"Pregnant," the psychiatrist said with disdain. "Why didn't you tell me that in the first place? That leaves me no choice. I'll call for an ambulance and send them to the address you gave me. You're both there at the moment, am I right?"

"Yes, you are right, but I'm not at all sure you're right about having her taken to the health center against her will. I guarantee there will be a physical struggle."

"That's what the paramedics are trained for—to manage these situations in a calm and sensible way, even with terrified patients who are convinced that they're being abducted."

"How should I prepare her for the paramedics?"

"Prepare her by not preparing her. Don't say anything about this until they arrive. They will take it from there. I will meet you and your wife at the health center."

"May I go with her in the ambulance?"

"If your presence calms her, yes. If she's upset by your presence, no."

In less than five minutes Earl saw the ambulance approaching the building. There was no siren wailing or lights flashing. He went down to the front door to let them in. Both the man and the woman were wearing thick blue jackets with arm-patches sewn on their right upper sleeve carrying the insignia of the ambulance company.

After introducing themselves, the man asked Earl, "Where is Mrs. Bromfman at the present time?"

"She's in her room with the door locked in our apartment on the fourth floor."

"All right, let's go up there, but before we do, this is what I'd like you to do when we get there. All three of us will try to be as quiet as humanly possible. We don't want to make her even more frightened than she already is. Then, you'll knock softly on the door to her room and ask if you can come in to talk with her. She'll probably say, 'About what?' Then you should say something like, 'About the two of us trying to figure things out. How to help you feel less frightened.' After that, anything can happen, and you'll have to do the best you can. We'll be right next to you and we may write things on a pad of paper or whisper to you. The cardinal rule is: do not lie. She will know immediately if you're lying to her, and then things can go downhill quickly. It is the truth that you and we are here to help her figure things out and feel less frightened, and we are doing everything we can to help her get to a place where she will feel safer. Do you have any questions for us?"

Earl said, "What will happen if she won't unlock the door to her bedroom?"

The female paramedic said, "That's a good question. It's a worst-case scenario. Since the room is a bedroom and not a closet, there has to be a window that is four storeys above the ground. So a desperate attempt to escape via the window is always a possibility. In order to avert severe bodily damage or death, we would have to break the door in. But we very rarely have to do that. Do you have any other questions?"

"No, I don't."

Outside Marta's bedroom, Earl knocked softly and said, "Marta, it's Earl. Are you all right?"

No answer.

"Marta, I'd like to talk to you."

Silence.

"Marta, I know that something terrible happened and that you're not sure who to trust, so it's hard to trust anything I say. But I hope that somewhere in you, you know that I would never do anything to hurt you."

No answer.

"Marta, just make a sound so I know you're in there and that I'm not talking to myself."

No response.

The male paramedic showed Earl a card on which he'd written, "A few more tries. It's not safe any longer."

Earl said, "Marta, I beg of you. Please let me in. I want to help you."

Earl made two more futile attempts before the male paramedic leaned against the door just hard enough to pull out the screws holding the old lock mechanism. He opened the door slowly. Marta was crouched on the floor in the far corner of the room with her knees pulled up to her chest. The female paramedic went in with Earl.

Earl said, "Marta, we need help. This lady and a kind man in the hallway will drive us to the health center so we can get some help there. I'll be with you the whole time."

Earl kneeled down so his head was just above Marta's. She pulled away. Her eyes were fearfully and angrily locked on his.

Earl said, "Let me help you up."

She leaned away again.

Earl said, "Let me just sit here next to you for a while. I'll ask this lady to wait outside in the hall."

The female paramedic left.

Earl sat on the floor with his side against Marta's. "You must be very tired. You need a safe place to rest. I promise I won't let anyone hurt you. I've never lied to you and I never will. Let's get up and we'll walk outside. The paramedics aren't going to hurt you. I promise."

Earl got back to his feet and put his hand out to Marta.

"Let me help you up."

Marta refused his hand and got to her feet on her own. Earl didn't dare touch her for fear she would feel that he was coercing her or worse. Once outside the building, Earl climbed into the back of the ambulance first and held his hand out to help Marta up the steps. She again refused his hand and climbed in herself. They sat down on the soft bench on the right side of the ambulance. Only then did the female paramedic get in with them. Marta's face was expressionless. The drive to the ambulance entrance of the health center took only a few minutes. The male paramedic drove very slowly.

A nurse at the health center was waiting outside for the ambulance. She introduced herself and escorted Earl and Marta to the interview room. As they entered the room, Dr. Hensley, who was sitting behind a wooden desk, stood and introduced himself. He invited them to have a seat in the two wooden chairs placed on the side of the desk opposite him. He had a more gentle demeanor than he had when Earl spoke with him on the phone. Marta was silent while Earl told the doctor what he knew and what he did not know. Dr. Hensley asked Marta how she was feeling. She looked blankly at him. He did not press her for a reply, instead telling them that he was going to leave them for a few minutes while he looked into what the bed situation was.

On returning, Dr. Hensley said that he would like Marta and Earl to come with him to meet the psychiatrist who would be working with Marta. Marta was now almost as lifeless as she had been when she staggered into the apartment the previous afternoon.

Dr. Hensley pressed the button outside two plastic-coated metal doors labeled Ward 3B. Someone inside buzzed them in. As they entered the ward, Earl found it a surprisingly comfortable space. There was brownish-tan carpeting—he had expected acres of shiny linoleum—and the furniture was made of wood, not plastic. The central room had windows on two sides. There were two corridors leading off the main room, where Earl presumed the bedrooms were located. The nurses' station, tucked into the corner closest to the door, was surrounded by a waist-high counter.

They were greeted by Dr. Anders, a petite, blonde of about fifty who spoke with an accent that sounded Scandinavian to Earl. She invited them to talk with her in her office, which was like the admissions office, but had two large windows and black-and-white nature photographs on the walls, along with Dr. Anders' diplomas. She addressed everything she said to both Earl and Marta, even after it became clear that Marta was unresponsive. It took more than an hour for Earl to answer all of Dr. Anders' questions. She then said that because of the risk of harm to the fetus, they could take no chances. Dr. Anders explained that she was going to put Marta on a three-day involuntary commitment, which could be extended to ten days if the situation warranted. She asked Marta if she understood her reasoning. Marta stared through the doctor. She asked the same of Earl, and he said he understood.

Dr. Anders said to Marta, "Your current state of fear and confusion could have been the result of a traumatic experience, but that is not always the case. It could have been brewing for years or could be a drug reaction."

Earl assured Dr. Anders that Marta had never taken any drugs and did not even drink alcohol.

Dr. Anders said that she would like to speak with Marta and Earl separately. She explained that she would start with Marta, so Earl should wait on the ward while she talked with his wife.

After Earl left, Dr. Anders said to Marta, "I will be your doctor while you're in the hospital, and afterwards if you'd like. We'll meet here in my office every day at least once, and, in addition, we'll meet whenever you feel it is a good idea for us to meet, even if we don't talk. You should feel free to speak, or be silent. You've introduced yourself to me in your own way, and you've made it clear to me that you're terrified. I know that you're feeling so frightened that you're cut off from words, and that you've all but given up on finding your way back to words and people. If you have any words or any other way of speaking to me, I'd welcome that, but I'll understand if you can't or don't want to."

Marta looked puzzled by Dr. Anders. Her eyes seemed to be asking the doctor if she could leave the room. Dr. Anders accompanied Marta to the nurses' station where a nurse dressed in ordinary street clothes said that she would show Marta the different parts of the ward.

Dr. Anders then nodded in Earl's direction indicating he should follow her to her office. She began by asking Earl if there was anything that he wanted to tell her but felt he could not say while Marta was present. Earl told her about they had decided to get married after Marta discovered that she was pregnant. He described Marta's extreme secrecy about, and isolation from, her family, and the unexpected appearance of her estranged sister in June, and the friendship that seemed to be developing between them.

When Dr. Anders began to form a picture in her mind of the life of this young couple, she said, "There are a number of things that I didn't want to discuss while Marta was here. First, breakdowns of the sort your wife is experiencing can be caused by physical illnesses of a great many types. We will be giving Marta a full medical work-up. If this is a drug reaction, the drug need not be a street drug; it could be a prescribed medication. Mr. Bromfman, please check at home for drugs—prescribed or otherwise. Also, because you've said that Marta is an extremely secretive person, please look carefully for anything that might point to a source of psychological trauma, such as records of doctor appointments that might be connected with a miscarriage or illness. Perhaps there have been family or academic problems that she has kept to herself. This is not a time to worry about being intrusive.

"There's another thing I didn't want to discuss while Marta was here. Because of the early stage of the pregnancy—we'll check hormone levels to determine the status of the pregnancy—I am loath to use any medications until we've had a chance to see how Marta responds to talking with the nursing staff and with me, and how she responds to the experience of being on the ward for a while. Some patients find the ward a safe place and feel very relieved to be here. Others feel as if they're being locked away in a prison, but of course those fears can change as time goes on. Now, do you have any questions of me?"

Earl paused and then said, "I know that you aren't a fortune teller, but if you have seen cases like Marta's, what are her chances of recovering from this?"

"I wish I could give you a definitive answer, but I can't. At this point, I can't even make a diagnosis. It will take some time for us to do that. And you have to remember that the experience that Marta is going through now, whatever its cause might be, is traumatic in its own right and that changes a person, as all traumas do. I apologize for using the technical term *trauma*. What I mean to say is that what Marta's going through now—whether it's a response to an actual event, like a rape or witnessing a murder, or imaginary, like the feeling that she's literally drowning in her own thoughts—is a terrible, life-changing experience in its own right."

After saying goodbye to Marta, who was staring blankly past him, Earl left the hospital through the large glass sliding doors at the front entrance. It was later than he had expected, deep into the evening. The streetlights were each surrounded by a globe of illuminated cold, damp air.

TEN

Randy Larsen was amazed by the dexterity with which he was dismissed by Anne, whose last name he learned from other guests at the funeral later in the day. He had never met a woman so self-possessed. As Randy thought about their exchange, he was embarrassed but also intrigued. He wished he had had the equanimity to say to her, "When would be a more suitable time to talk?" He fussed over the words he might have used—would the phrase "more suitable time" have made him sound like a hayseed deputy attempting to sound "educated"? He considered and rejected the idea of following her after the reception or having another deputy follow her. It was as difficult to place her in relation to Marta's death as it was to place Earl. He had observed that she and Earl had not yet said a word to one another or even acknowledged one another's presence. It's not unusual for a person not to be on speaking terms with a relative. But this woman was the only member of Marta's family to attend her funeral, which, to Randy, suggested a division in the family in which she and Marta, and perhaps Earl, were on the same side of that divide. When Randy spoke to Marta's father on the phone, Mr. Noel showed not the least inclination to attend his daughter's funeral, and said he didn't know if his younger daughter, in her early thirties, was still alive. This woman is not supposed to exist. Neither Earl nor his children mentioned that Marta had a sister. And yet, she's not in hiding. Quite the opposite. She dresses in a way that draws attention in a highly effective, understated way.

There was something that one of the deputies who searched Earl's house had turned up which, like so many other aspects of this case, did not sit right with Randy—it was now very definitely a "case" in Randy's mind. The deputy, during the search of Earl's house, had found recent bills for electricity, gas, feed, tractor parts, and the like, as well as Marta's pay stubs from the diner. What he had not found was a recent telephone bill. When asked about this, Earl explained that he throws away bills that he has paid unless he needs them for his business records.

With Earl's permission, the deputy requested from the telephone company a record of the calls made from Earl's house during the past three months. The records were delivered promptly. It turned out that in the two days following Marta's death, there were two calls made from Earl's home phone to a number with a Chicago area code. They were long calls made late at night, and they were expensive. No long distance calls had been made in the months prior to Marta's death. In Randy's mind, the calls could only have been made to Anne. He figured that Earl would not have risked calling Anne while Marta was still alive for fear of her overhearing him talking or noticing the charges on the phone bill.

Randy's mind kept churning. If Earl had made calls to Anne while Marta was still alive, they most likely were collect calls made from the public phone booths closest to the Bromfman farm. Those phone records would be more difficult to get, but it could be done. Randy wondered if his "conspiracy theory" was fomented by a need to avenge himself for having been made to feel like a pathetic hick posturing as a detective.

Earl, too, was preoccupied with Anne. She had filled the entire church when she stepped in the front door. Anne's presence was the only thing that felt real and alive to him. But at the same time, he had a feeling that he had lived his life and that it was too late for anything to change in a way that mattered. He had been forced prematurely into adulthood by getting Marta pregnant and marrying her. He had raised two children in the same house with Marta—which is not to say that he and Marta had raised the children together—and now he was burying her. The cycle of Marta's entry into his life, and exit from it, was now complete. Anne had played a central role in that life with Marta, a life that was lived, and was now over.

And yet it was evident to Earl that he was not dead, that his life had not ended with Marta's. He was no less moved by Anne now than he had been sixteen years earlier when he first met her. Also, as real now as it was when it occurred, was the dense sadness he felt on returning to the attic apartment the night that Marta was hospitalized at the University Health Center. It was almost eleven at night, almost Sunday morning. The apartment was quieter than it ever had been. It seemed surreal to him at the time to think that earlier that same day, he and the two paramedics had stood in the hallway trying to get a response from Marta, who might have already killed herself by jumping out of the fourth storey bedroom window. It would not have surprised Earl in the least if she had killed herself. Marta was no longer Marta; she was a woman who seemed hardly a person at all. Earl felt he had to talk to someone, and he thought there was no one but Anne with whom to talk without betraying Marta's privacy. He wondered, even then, if he was using Marta's breakdown as a way to justify calling Anne.

When Anne picked up the phone, words poured from Earl's mouth. "Anne, Marta is in the hospital now. She's had some kind of mental collapse. When she got home for supper yesterday, she looked like a zombie. Her face was without expression. She didn't talk and she could hardly stand. I helped her get to her bed and I lay next to her all night hoping she'd be better after some sleep. But when she woke up she was worse. She didn't believe I was who I claimed to be. I called the University Health Center and they had a psychiatrist call me here. After I told him what had happened, he called an ambulance. The paramedics were here and took her to a locked psychiatric ward. I was in the ambulance with her. She didn't seem to know who I was or who she was or what an ambulance was."

"Earl, back up. Tell me what happened from the beginning, slowly. There's no rush."

"That's right, there's no rush."

"So take it slowly. Just start at the beginning."

Earl told the story for the fourth time that day, but it had not become rote. Each time he told it, he saw it from a different angle, and so he told it differently. This time he told the story not to tell Marta's story, but to tell the story of what happened to him that day. They talked for more than two hours, both of them feeling the freedom of being able to say everything they wanted to say, and ask everything they wanted to ask. Time presented no limitation.

A few days after Marta entered the hospital, Dr. Anders told Earl that he could come see Marta during visiting hours. She cautioned him not to expect dramatic change. He visited every day. During the visits, Marta sat motionless and expressionless in one of the chairs in the open area of the ward while Earl sat near her. Their two chairs seemed to be floating in the middle of an ocean with no sign of land, no direction in which to head. Sometimes he tried talking to her about things he had read in the newspaper, not expecting a response and not getting one. At other times, he just sat silently with her. After a few weeks, a striking change in Marta occurred, seemingly overnight between two of Earl's daily visits: her body, which had been limp and lifeless, became increasingly tense. Her knuckles now were white as her hands gripped the arms of the chair in which she was sitting, her jaw muscles protruded as she clenched her teeth. The look in her eye was no longer as vacant as that of a dead bird; her eyes met his, but met them in condemnation. For what, he didn't know. Maybe just for being him.

Earl did not say anything to Marta about this change, but he told Dr. Anders that he was worried that Marta was getting worse, becoming paranoid and crazy the way she had been when he first called the health center.

Dr. Anders said, "I think what you're noticing is a reflection of Marta's gradually coming to life, returning to the world of the living. But the world she's coming back to is still a terrifying place, a place that she hates. The good news is that if anything of importance has occurred during her stay here, the world she's returning to isn't exactly the same place as the one she left. It may be a little less frightening and a little less worthy of her hatred."

The idea that Marta was frightened and enraged was not a surprise to Earl. He had known that since the first day he met her. But something must have happened to push her over the edge on the day of her breakdown. In the weeks since his first meeting with Dr. Anders, Earl had been putting off searching the apartment for clues that might shed light on what had been going on in Marta's life just before her breakdown.

The prospect of violating Marta's privacy, which was so important to her, made Earl feel nauseous, but he finally went ahead anyway. Earl looked at her datebook and at the letters and bills on her desk and in her knapsack, and he went through her closet and dresser drawers, but found nothing out of the ordinary. After an hour, he decided to clear his head by taking a walk around the campus in the brisk morning air. On returning to the apartment, while hanging his coat on the coat rack opposite the front door, he noticed Marta's winter coat. She had been wearing that loden coat when she arrived at the apartment in a daze that Friday afternoon, and she had worn it when she left the apartment for her short walk the next morning, but she was not wearing a coat when she got into the ambulance. Earl checked both pockets of Marta's coat and found a crumpled letter addressed to her from the Office of the Comptroller dated two days before her breakdown. The letter surprised him. Apparently, the comptroller's office had found a problem connected with her financial aid package and had asked her in an accusatory way to make an appointment to answer their questions.

Earl immediately knew in his bones what had happened. He was convinced that someone in the comptroller's office had caught Marta in a lie and had used the lie to humiliate her and perhaps blackmail her. For Marta, no torture could be more diabolically effective than threatening to reveal to the world one of her secrets. He had no doubt that Marta was capable of killing herself or the person holding her hostage.

Earl paced the hallway of the apartment, gripping the letter as tightly as his thoughts gripped him. He imagined going to the health center and showing Dr. Anders the letter, but he dismissed the idea—he could handle this himself. Showing the letter to Marta would only compound her humiliation—she would feel that there was no one on earth who did not know her secret. Earl imagined barging into the comptroller's office to confront Francine Gallagher with the damage she had done. He would be viewed as a hysterical husband looking for someone to blame for his wife's insanity. But what else was there to do but confront the person who humiliated Marta? Was it conceivable that Francine Gallagher was a kindly woman who was simply trying to help Marta, and that Marta had put herself in her own imaginary pillory? No, it did not seem possible. The state that Marta was in when she returned to the apartment late that afternoon was unlike anything he had ever seen. He felt convinced that Marta had not jumped off a cliff, she had been pushed. So he decided to talk to Miss Gallagher.

When he arrived at the long counter in the comptroller's office at which Marta had stood weeks earlier, he was calm and observant. Other students had formed a short line as they waited.

When it was his turn, Earl said, "I'd like to speak to Miss Gallagher."

The woman behind the counter said, "Would you tell me what you need from the comptroller's office, so I can point you in the right direction?"

"I've come in response to a letter from Francine Gallagher requesting that some matter be cleared up. The letter wasn't specific."

"Your name please."

"Earl Bromfman, B-r-o-m-f-m-a-n."

The woman said, "Wait here for just a moment."

She walked to a desk in the far left corner of the room where she leaned down to speak into the ear of the dour, middle-aged woman sitting at the desk. They talked for a minute or so before the woman from the front desk straightened up and walked back to the counter with a worried look on her face.

"Please have a seat, Mr. Bromfman. Miss Gallagher is busy at the moment but will be with you as soon as possible." Gesturing toward one of the long backless benches, she said, "Please have a seat."

Earl felt certain that Marta had been asked to sit on the same set of benches. His mind was clear in a way that he had never before experienced. There was no background noise in his head. Visual images were crisp—the outlines of objects precise, as if drawn with the sharpest of instruments. Colors were vibrant.

Time passed—Earl had no idea how much time—before the woman at the front counter said, "Mr. Bromfman, Miss Gallagher is ready to see you now."

Earl rose, walked slowly, deliberately, to the corner desk where Miss Gallagher, with only the movement of her eyes, instructed Earl to sit in the black wooden chair on the opposite side of her desk. With the slightest nod of her head in his direction, she wordlessly asked Earl to explain what he wanted from her.

"My wife, Marta Bromfman, was here to see you on December thirteenth of last year."

Earl paused, waiting for Miss Gallagher to confirm that this was so. She offered no such confirmation, and instead looked at him as if to say, what of it?

He continued, "She was here in response to a letter she received from you asking that she come in to clear up a problem that had arisen concerning her financial aid package."

Again, Miss Gallagher sat waiting for a question.

"Do you recall meeting with my wife?"

Miss Gallagher sighed as if resenting the tedium of dealing with petty matters that should have been filtered out long before they reached her. "Yes, I remember meeting with your wife. Would you please get to the point."

Earl, still lucid in a way that felt almost surreal, said, "Would you please tell me what occurred at that meeting?"

"I would think that that's your wife's business, not yours. She has postponed dealing with this matter for a very long time. If she has any further questions, by all means tell her to make another appointment with the Office of the Comptroller."

"I'm here and not my wife because immediately after her meeting with you, she had a mental breakdown and she's been hospitalized at the University Health Center for the past five weeks, completely mute. Only today did I find the letter you sent her, and I'm here to find out what happened in the meeting you had with her."

"Since you are her husband, and she is apparently unable to deal with this matter herself, I will tell you what occurred. I informed your wife that an audit had turned up

148

an inconsistency in her father's signature on her financial aid forms. I was simply the messenger, but people from time immemorial have been disposed to killing the messenger."

"Would you tell me the tenor of that meeting?"

"It was some time ago. As I remember it, Mrs. Bromfman at first side-stepped the forgeries on the financial aid forms, but then admitted to having forged her father's signature. All that seemed quite straightforward. What seemed to unsettle her was the fact that the comptroller's office had made its own inquiries, and in talking with her father, had found that he had not signed any financial aid applications—I believe there were seven forgeries in all over a period of four years."

Earl sat quietly for a few moments, his mind still strangely clear.

He said, "Miss Gallagher, both of us know that you are lying by omission. What you're leaving out of your account is the immense pleasure you took in flaying my wife, whose agony was clearly visible to you. You took particular pleasure then, as I could see in your face a few moments ago, in delivering the deathblow—the fact that you had informed her father that she had forged his signature—as if it were just another detail of no greater significance than all the others. I can only imagine how delicious that moment was for you—you and her father, bound together in the delight of causing pain that quietly, efficiently brought my wife down. You felt the thrill of checkmate in a game in which you pretended to be merely an observer—the 'messenger,' as you put it. I wonder how someone like you lives with herself—perhaps by blinding yourself to who you are by means of a continuous series of lies, self-deceptions that you actually believe, most of the time. There must be still hours in the night when your lies are no longer credible, even to you, and you share in some of the pain you've brought to so many over the years. Shame on you, Miss Gallagher, shame on you."

Francine Gallagher was struck dumb. She had never been spoken to in such an insolent way. Earl stood, not taking his eyes from hers, pushed his chair back, and then turned and walked to the dark oak door of the comptroller's office. His heart was not pounding, his knees were not wobbling, his mind had never been so clear.

Earl walked for a long time, crisscrossing the campus deep in thought. He felt somehow complete, but not triumphant, for he was well aware that he had not succeeded in changing anything. He was not so naïve as to think that he had undone or set right the damage that had been done. That had not been his intent. What then, had been his intent? To punish Miss Gallagher? It couldn't be done. To elicit an apology or a sign of concern from her? Impossible. Saying what should be said to the person to whom it should be said—that was what he wanted to believe had been his motive. But, if he was to be honest with himself, he did not know why he had spoken to Miss Gallagher as he had. Oddly enough, he hadn't been frightened. He had not rehearsed what he was going to say to her. In fact, he had not known what he would say until he heard the words come from his mouth. He was glad that he had done what he had done, but he knew that, for her, he was merely a self-righteous adolescent having a temper tantrum, which was to be expected now and again when working at a university. She no doubt saw him as an overgrown boy who needed someone to blame for his poor judgment in marrying so young, and in choosing a mentally ill woman to be his wife.

Earl doubted that he would ever tell Marta about this encounter with Miss Gallagher—why was he calling her Miss Gallagher? He sounded like a fourth grader talking about his schoolteacher. What he had done, he did because it was the right thing to do—right because it felt right to him. He wanted very badly to believe that. As he continued to walk, he wept with sadness for Marta. She had suffered far more than any person should suffer. She did not deserve it, but as far as he could tell, deserving and suffering rarely have anything to do with each other.

150

Earl slept soundly that night for the first time since Marta's breakdown more than a month earlier. The next morning Earl called Dr. Anders' secretary to see if he could meet with her for a few minutes that afternoon. They met in an office off the ward so that Marta would not think that they were conspiring against her or that Dr. Anders was telling Earl the secrets that Dr. Anders had learned by reading Marta's mind.

Earl began by handing Dr. Anders the letter from Francine Gallagher that he had found in Marta's coat pocket. As she read it, he told her that he had spoken with Miss Gallagher and that she had told him that she had met with Marta on the day that Marta came home in a state of mental and physical collapse. Miss Gallagher said that Marta had at first tried to evade confessing to forging her father's signature on the financial aid forms, but then admitted to having done so. She had then told Marta that she had spoken to Marta's father, and he denied having signed the forms. This humiliated and frightened Marta in the worst possible way. Earl said he did not know if Miss Gallagher had threatened Marta with expulsion from the university or arrest for forgery or some other charge.

Earl and Dr. Anders sat in silence after he finished telling her what he had learned. In that silence, Earl had the feeling—and he suspected that Dr. Anders did as well—that he had uncovered information that had a direct bearing on Marta's breakdown, but what he had learned did not change anything at all. He knew Marta so well that he had known from the outset that something had happened that had caused Marta to feel exposed and terribly humiliated. Exactly what form that exposure had taken he had not known, but it didn't really matter. It struck Earl at that moment that in detective stories, there is always the unearthing of a clue that leads to the villain's arrest, and the arrest of the villain returns the lives of the characters to a state exactly as it had been before the villain committed his crime. He now realized that he had believed, because he had wanted to believe, that people could be "all right"—meaning the same as before—after horrific things had been done to them.

Dr. Anders broke the silence by saying, "Thank you for doing all you've done in putting together a picture of what happened the afternoon of Marta's breakdown. The more we know about what Marta's been through the less she has to be alone with it."

Earl said, "I think that Marta's been alone for so long now that she will always be alone no matter what you or I or anyone else knows."

In the months that followed, Marta voluntarily remained on the psychiatric ward of the University Health Center—which, in light of her mutism, is only to say that she made no effort and wrote no request to leave. Dr. Anders prepared the forms for Marta to file for a medical leave from the university. Marta's pregnancy was monitored closely; the high doses of anti-psychotic and anti-depressant medications that Dr. Anders prescribed were, according to Dr. Anders, "of no known danger to the fetus"—whatever that means. Earl was unsure whether Marta was aware that she was pregnant.

ELEVEN

In the weeks immediately following Marta's breakdown, Earl felt so depleted that he could do little more than attend some of his classes, visit Marta, and sleep. He spoke with Anne by phone a couple of times a week. During this period, Anne broached what she felt to be a delicate matter. "I know you have a lot to handle and I don't want to add to the load you're carrying. And I don't want to be intrusive. I know it will sound horribly selfish when I say this, but I feel extremely lonely. It feels as if I've lost the only real friends I've ever had. Would you consider letting me continue to visit on the weekends the way I've been doing since the beginning of the summer? I know that it might look to others as if I'm trying to steal my sister's husband while she's in the hospital. That's all. It was hard to ask you that."

There was a long silence during which the static on the phone line seemed to increase in volume. Earl, too, was concerned that Anne's spending the weekends alone with him in the apartment would appear shamelessly lascivious and a terrible betrayal of Marta. If Marta knew, she would no doubt blow a fuse. But he was sick of worrying about what would or would not upset Marta. He vowed at that moment not to allow Marta's insanity to dictate how he lived his life. What occurred between him and Anne was his responsibility, and he would answer to himself, and to nobody else, for it.

He said to Anne, "It will be good to see you."

Even though Anne had a key to the apartment and had let herself in on many occasions in the course of the previous eight months, she knocked on the door to the apartment. After some initial awkwardness, she and Earl adjusted to being alone in the apartment with one another. It was a welcome change for Earl to be able to talk openly about whatever he wanted, whenever he wanted, and to get an honest and thoughtful response in return. And Anne felt enormously grateful to Earl for allowing her to resume being a part of the life he had made with Marta. As flawed as that life was, it was the best family she had ever been a part of.

As had been immediately apparent to Earl in his first encounter with Anne the previous June, not only was she enormously sexy, she had a very quick mind, far faster than his. He was free to enjoy her intelligence and her wit, but her sexiness presented a major dilemma now that they, for all intents and purposes, were living together, and were no longer subject to Marta's vigilant eye.

Earl, who had not thought of himself as capable of being amusing, much less funny, found that he and Anne, without being aware of it, had developed a way of turning ordinary situations into vaudeville routines. One afternoon he and Anne were talking while listening to music in the living room. Earl got up to leave the room. As he made his way to the door, she said, "Would you shut the door?" He shot back without missing a beat, "'Would you shut the door' *what*?" Picking up the cue, she said, "Would you shut the door *now*!" They found this extraordinarily funny, as two people in love are wont to do.

Though Earl and Anne were spending every weekend together, Anne used Marta's bedroom and Earl used his. They could, in one sense, honestly say that they had no sexual relationship. Never once did they kiss or even hold hands. But they both knew that it was not true that they did not have a sexual relationship. Only occasionally did their arms or shoulders brush against one another as they walked together or prepared a meal in the kitchen, but when this inadvertent touching of bodies occurred, the sensations that ran through each of them were nothing less than explosive, though they both pretended that nothing out of the ordinary had occurred. Their sexual relationship was fully alive in myriad other ways: in the timbre of Earl's voice as he said Anne's name; in the erotic dance Anne performed—a dance more sexy than the tango—as she hopped on one bare foot and slipped a shoe on the other foot, which she raised behind her (no male is able to perform this dance, Earl would say to himself); and perhaps most exciting of all, the amazingly arousing movement of Anne's right hand brushing back and tucking behind her ear the unruly lock of hair that time and again slipped forward across her eye (the consummate feminine gesture, Earl thought). A sexual relationship of this type is as old as the human race, and is at least as sensuous and exciting as anything that can occur between two people in bed. Anne and Earl could allow the sexual relationship to burn white-hot because they both knew, or thought they knew, that neither of them would ever allow it to become sexual in the customary forms.

In the course of Earl's daily visits to Marta, she very gradually became able to look at him, though not in the eye. When she finally uttered a word to him, she directed it to the floor. Earl never asked questions. He said things that he hoped she would not find at all intrusive, but he found that this was more difficult than he had anticipated. When he mentioned the forced resignation of the president of the university, he immediately wished he could somehow take the words back into his mouth. Of course, Marta would feel that he was making indirect reference to *her* disgrace, *her* leaving the university.

She fell silent and refused to see him when he came to visit the next two days. As was characteristic of Earl, after these rebuffs, he got up, brushed himself off, and tried again. Marta depended on him to be able to do that, and he never disappointed her.

Walking to the University Health Center each day, Earl, with the eye of a farmer, noticed the subtle reflections of the change of seasons. In late February, he watched the transformations of the quiet snowdrifts that had covered the vast expanses of campus lawn. The plains of snow were reduced to tawdry islands of brown, grainy ice surrounded by moats of watery mud. In the thin margins between the ice and the mud, shoots of grass reached through the thick water toward the portion of cloud cover that was back-lit by the sun. An occasional patch of pale blue shone through the gaps between the continents of clouds, a welcome change from the impenetrable, purple-black clouds of winter. By mid-March, the earth had swallowed the remaining snow, as well as the ice and mud. In their place was emerald green grass that sparkled in the first sustained sunlight in half a year. For Earl there was a feeling of loss in watching the trees burst with buds that would soon become a profusion of leaves behind which the large, muscular limbs of the trees that etched black abstract drawings in the winter sky would become mere supporting actors in the ostentatious display.

Sequestered in the ward for months now, Marta would have no truck with reality, particularly the reality of her pregnancy. At first she pretended it was not happening. She submitted to the examinations by Dr. Warner, one of the University Medical Center's obstetricians, without acknowledging his existence. When Marta was no longer able to fasten the waist of her trousers due to the protrusion of her abdomen, she became irate, blaming the laundry service for shrinking her clothes. When the weight of reality became too great for her to carry, Marta sunk into despair. For Earl, Marta's despair felt like a resurgence of the person whom he recognized as Marta.

The first substantive statement that Marta made during Earl's visits was, "I'm going to have a baby that I don't want to have."

Earl said, "I know. But you and I will make a good family for this baby."

Marta yelled into Earl's face, "Stop being the perennial Boy Scout. I can't stand it." With that she stood and stalked off to her room.

A few days later, on returning to the apartment at the end of the day, Earl checked his mailbox and Marta's. There was another letter to Marta from the Office of the Comptroller, which he read.

> *Dear Mrs. Bromfman,*
>
> *In light of the fact that you are on medical leave from the University, we will defer further discussion of the concerns we have raised until such time as you next register for classes at the University.*
>
> *Sincerely,*
> *Francine Gallagher*
> *Assistant Comptroller*

Earl found the letter to be diabolically perfect. In effect Miss Gallagher was telling Marta that if she ever dared try to complete her degree, the Office of the Comptroller would unleash its fury upon her by reopening the inquiry into the forgeries. They could be quite certain that Marta would never put herself through that, so in effect, she was being banned from the university, and probably from every other university in the country. What made Francine Gallagher's letter perfect was the fact that she delivered this permanent ban of Marta from higher education in the form of a one-sentence statement that pretended to be motivated by a wish to diminish Marta's worries while she was recovering from her breakdown. The effect of the letter, as Earl saw it, was that of indelibly marking Marta with still another source of shame that she would hold secret for the rest of her life.

Earl was correct in his assessment. Marta did not graduate from college or pursue higher education of any sort, never worked in a capacity other than that of a farmer's wife and a waitress in a diner, and never spoke a word to anyone about the shame of the exposure of her forgeries.

Unlike the intensity of his reaction to reading Francine Gallagher's letter months earlier, this time Earl felt not the slightest impulse to confront Miss Gallagher about her relentless cruelty or to inform Dr. Anders of this development. He knew that time had long ago run out for hope, or even for what satisfaction could be had, in protest or outrage. The cards had been dealt, and he, Marta, Anne, and the baby would have to do the best they could with the cards they were holding.

Anne arrived for the weekend two days after Earl read the letter from the comptroller's office. This particular Friday evening was different in that Earl was ill at ease. Anne noticed but did not say anything. After the dishes were washed and put in the drying rack, they went to the living room to listen to one of the albums that Anne had brought.

As she looked through the albums, deciding which to play first, Earl said, "Anne, would you sit down because I want to say something to you."

Anne looked worried as she put the albums aside. Earl was already seated at one end of the weathered, brown corduroy couch. Anne took a seat at the other end.

Earl looked at Anne plaintively for a few moments before saying, "I'm afraid I'm going to make a fool of myself and worse by saying something to you that I've wanted to say for months now …"

Anne interrupted, "I think I know what you're going to say, but I think that it will make things harder than they already are if you say it. Nothing can happen between us beyond what we're doing now, and even that will have to stop when Marta

158

gets out of the hospital. She's my sister and your wife, and she's going to have your baby in a few months."

Earl protested, "Let me finish. I have to say it now because if I don't it will never get said and I couldn't bear to go for the rest of my life without saying it at least once. I'm in love with you. I fell in love with you when we first talked on the landing outside the apartment, and I've been in love with you ever since. Whatever happens, I won't ever regret having had this time with you. I know I sound like a love-struck boy, but I hope you won't laugh at me in your mind. I know that I'll never meet anyone who is remotely like you, and I would give anything to spend the rest of my life with you. God this sounds trite. I wish I had better words for what I'm trying to say. It has also been agony for me not knowing how you feel about me. I'm pretty sure that you like me, but I'm afraid that you like me as a friend, and nothing more. I know that you're Marta's sister and I'm her husband, but those facts don't change anything about the way I feel about you. I had to tell you."

Anne paused for what felt like several minutes, but probably was only five or ten seconds, before saying, "My dear, dear Earl." She looked into his big eyes in his big face. "It didn't happen for me as quickly as it did for you, but I have fallen in love with you. I'm afraid that saying it out loud will bring the world down on top of us. It's wrong for us to be in love. I don't mean church-wrong, or Romeo-and-Juliet-wrong, I mean that it's a terrible thing to do to Marta. Neither of us could live with ourselves if you divorced her and left her alone with the baby, or if we had an affair. And, aside from what's right and wrong, I wouldn't want to be the woman on the side who doesn't get to have a family of her own. I know that that sounds cold and calculating, but we're talking about something real, not a daydream. I'm sorry that this conversation has to end on such a hard note. I don't want to destroy what we have, but I also don't want it to become anything different from what it is."

Earl's face collapsed into tears when Anne finished. He covered his face with his two large hands, and leaned forward until his hands and face were pressed against his knees. Anne moved to Earl's end of the couch, put her arm half-way around his broad shoulders, and pressed her forehead against the top of his head. Earl sobbed, choking on the salty mixture of tears and mucus that he drew in with each breath. He had never in his life felt such pain—pain that seemed to be housed in his chest and throat, but held no resemblance to physical pain. Anne's arm around him, and her forehead against the side of his head, were neither exciting nor comforting. He could feel her pity, but she was already much farther away than she had been an hour earlier. When he straightened up and looked at her, he was surprised to see tears running down her face. But they were tears of sorrow for him, he thought, not tears born of her own pain.

Earl spoke with Dr. Anders every week or so for ten or fifteen minutes. The unusually lengthy hospitalization, Dr. Anders explained, was due to what she saw as the high risk of suicide and other forms of harm to the baby. In recent weeks she and Earl had talked about the fact that Marta would need time after leaving the hospital to re-acclimate to the outside world and to prepare herself and her home for the birth of the baby. Earl knew full well that Marta, even under the best of circumstances, would not be capable of caring for an infant. There would be only a month or five weeks between the birth in late April or early May and Earl's graduation at the beginning of June. He had asked his mother if she would stay with Marta and him for the period between the birth of the baby and his graduation. She'd told Earl that she would be glad to help out for those weeks, but wondered what he had in mind for his family after he graduated. Earl's heart sank as he asked her if it would be all right if he and Marta and the baby lived at the farm for a while. He said that he would work with his father, who had been stretched to his limits since Earl's older

160

brother had left the farm to work in Indiana. Not only did this plan postpone—perhaps a euphemism for end—Earl's dream of becoming an engineer, it also acknowledged the fact that Marta would not be graduating from the university and going on to pursue her hope of becoming a restorer of rare books, and instead would be returning to life on a small farm, a fate she once thought she had succeeded in escaping.

Earl's mother said that he and his family were always welcome to live at the farm for as long as they wanted. He and Marta and the baby would live in the room that Earl, Leslie, and Paul had slept in when they were growing up. Unspoken, but audible in Earl's voice, was the disappointment he felt in giving up his dreams of becoming an engineer. He had never imagined that he would be asking to return to the place and the life that he had wanted so much to leave. Another kind of sadness that Earl's mother heard, but could not name, was Earl's sadness about the prospect of living without Anne.

Dr. Anders had taken a particular interest in Marta right from the beginning of the hospitalization. This was subliminally evident to Earl and very clear to the ward staff. Ordinarily, after the intake interviews, Dr. Anders would transfer the patient to a staff psychiatrist, who would take charge of the subsequent treatment of the patient. Dr. Anders was liked and respected by the hospital staff, but her position as the chair of the Department of Psychiatry and a member of the board of the University Medical Center made her a daunting figure. Her decisions almost always went unquestioned, at least openly. Marta, for most of her stay in the hospital, was so withdrawn as to be oblivious to all of this. She subsisted in a world inside of herself populated by the wraiths of a former life. The gossip on the ward had it that Marta held special importance for Dr. Anders because Marta, like Dr. Anders, came from a Swedish immigrant family. Dr. Anders, now in her fifties, had never married and was childless. Marta's soon-to-be-born baby, so the gossip went, was Dr. Anders' baby that never was.

It was highly unusual for a patient to remain on the ward for more than a month. Only one or two members of the nursing staff could remember a hospital stay as long as Marta's. Dr. Anders met with Marta each day for anywhere from fifteen minutes to an hour. For the first three or four weeks, Marta was silent for the entirety of the sessions. Dr. Anders put no pressure on Marta to speak, and instead sat silently with Marta, occasionally talking to her about thoughts that came to mind while sitting with Marta.

In one of these meetings, Dr. Anders said, "Despite what most people say, not everybody wants to be understood."

She paused for a few minutes before going on.

"You and I know that being understood can be a very dangerous thing. It gives people power over us that we don't want them to have."

A few minutes later, she continued, "One of the scariest movies I've ever seen was a film I saw when I was about seven. It's much too old a film for you to have seen. I recall vividly the scene in which a girl is forced into a spaceship by aliens whose faces you never see, but that makes them even scarier because you imagine the most horrible faces possible. She is hooked up to a machine that takes her earthling life out of her and puts into her another life, an alien life. The writer of the movie knew something very important: people can have their lives stolen from them. I don't think that there's anything worse that can happen to a person. It's the scariest thing there is, at least for me."

Marta, whose eyes had been fixed to the floor in an unfocused way, looked up at Dr. Anders for a moment and then lowered her eyes again.

The following afternoon, when Dr. Anders arrived on the ward for her meeting with Marta, a nurse said that Marta had refused to get out of bed that morning, and despite concerted effort on the part of the staff, she was still in bed with the blankets pulled up over her head. Dr. Anders said, "That's good news. I'll go tell her I'll be in my office waiting for her so she can register her protest against me more directly."

Very gradually over the course of the succeeding weeks, Marta became increasingly stubborn, refusing to eat or bathe or get out of bed. She spawned a foul odor that made it repulsive to stand near her for any length of time. Dr. Anders aired out her office after meeting with Marta, but the odor never completely disappeared. The acrid smell seemed to have seeped into the fabric of the chairs and curtains in the office. Dr. Anders was deeply disturbed by this, feeling that Marta had made her way into her body and into her personal life far beyond what she had given Marta permission to do. Though she never told anyone, Dr. Anders bought odor-removal products at the hardware store and scrubbed the curtains and the cushion of the chair in which Marta sat in an effort to rid herself of Marta's stench. As time went on, Dr. Anders became convinced that the odor had seeped into the clothes she wore while with Marta, clothes that were very important to the identity of this stylish Swedish doctor.

The ward staff was not used to dealing with patients who overstayed their welcome to the degree Marta was overstaying hers, nor were they used to the insanity with which a patient like Marta could saturate the air the nurses breathed eight hours a day, week in and week out. Many grew to hate Marta and deeply resent Dr. Anders, who could just waltz in and out of the ward as she pleased because she was "oh so important," while they were confined to a ward that had been transformed from a place they enjoyed into a dungeon in which they merely did their time. Neither did the staff concur with Dr. Anders' belief that Marta was returning to the land of the living by means of her violent and malodorous assault on the peacefulness of a place in which they once felt they were actually helping people.

The nursing staff eventually became so upset by what was happening that they dared to tell Dr. Anders that they thought

Marta had gotten as much help from the hospitalization as she could, and that she should be sent home to be cared for by her family, as was the practice with the other students who were hospitalized. Dr. Anders talked with the staff about her observation that Marta was getting better in the sense that she was no longer the ghost she had been when she was admitted. Her odor and her other forms of stubbornness were lifesaving for her, they were assaults on her childhood family that had been far more toxic than the smelly toilet that she was turning the ward into.

The staff was not in the mood for theories and did not feel the least bit inclined to play the role of the toilet for Marta's childhood problems, even if these problems were unthinkably horrible. After the feelings of the staff were voiced, and Dr. Anders responded to them as best she could, nothing changed. Dr. Anders was adamant that Marta could not be discharged in her current state: she had no family to whose care she could be discharged, she was still a serious suicidal risk, and she could not be entrusted with the life of the fetus whose existence she seemed to loathe.

Months passed, and to the begrudging recognition of the ward staff, Marta's rage subsided and she began to accept help from the people who were there to help her. This was really all that the staff wanted—to be seen as people who have value. And it was precisely that recognition that, for Marta, had been most important to withhold.

As the tide of insanity ebbed, two realities became inescapable for all concerned, including Marta: Marta was in her third trimester of pregnancy, her abdomen protruding, her breasts engorged; and she would have to leave the hospital in order to care for the baby once it was born. Negotiating Marta's re-entry into the world outside of the hospital, and the reentry of that world into Marta, were of paramount importance. Marta finally agreed to read letters from Anne that she had previously pushed away. They were letters in which Anne said she missed Marta and looked forward to seeing her. The letters brought back frightening childhood memories, but the images did not undo Marta.

Marta began to take walks outside of the hospital with Earl. The first walk lasted only a few minutes before Marta became so anxious that she begged Earl to take her back to the ward. The following day—a brisk, clear morning, with a fine mist in the air—they cautiously walked through the parking lot of the hospital. For Marta, everything was too much. The daylight was blinding and the sky was expansive, pulling her up into its immensity. The cars on the street moved faster and faster as they approached, then became a solid, sustained, brightly colored flash, and finally disappeared into the horizon.

Marta and Earl crossed the street onto the campus, which was quieter, but no less an assault on Marta's sensorium: the grass was glistening as if crawling with sheets of shiny insects, the trees were too jagged, their branches pointing Marta in a thousand directions at once; the students walking near her were speaking in languages she couldn't understand. Marta's heart was pounding. She stopped, closed her eyes tightly, put her palms over her ears, and shrieked. Earl put his arms around her waist and pulled her close to him. He said, "It's all new. You'll get used to it. You will. Let's just stand here a while." She pushed Earl away, but then wrapped both of her arms tightly around his right arm.

Earl had no particular route in mind. They seemed to move as if propelled by an invisible current carrying them from one path to the next, until they arrived at the building where they had lived in the attic apartment together such a very long time ago. To Marta, it looked like a faded, creased, black-and-white photo of a building in a foreign city where an elderly relative had once lived. A number of broken and rusting gutters draped the front to the brick building like macabre metal vines. The entranceway was dark and musty. Many of the aluminum doors of the line of mailboxes had been broken off, leaving dark holes that looked like missing teeth in a gigantic, metallic mouth. The climb up the four flights of stairs felt vaguely familiar to Marta. She knew that she was not the same person who had once climbed these stairs.

On entering the apartment, Marta stood frozen in place for a minute or two. Without saying a word, she then walked down the hall to the door of the kitchen where she stood for some minutes, seemingly attempting to remember who she was when she occupied this space. She then re-entered the hallway, took a few steps, and stood at the threshold of the living room as if looking deep into the face of someone she felt she once knew, but could not quite remember. Marta proceeded down the hallway, peering into each room as if trying to locate herself in relation to it. When she stepped into the bathroom at the end of the hall, she seemed to be at war with herself, taking a step forward and then back, again and again. Finally, she took a forceful step straight ahead and looked down into the sink. She then pulled the shower curtain aside and scanned the inside of the bathtub. She then proceeded more rapidly to examine the contents of the medicine chest and the cabinet below the sink. With explosive force, she turned and ran down the hall-way with her eyes fixed on Earl's. She threw herself against his chest, which collision barely moved his body. Earl tried to get his arms around Marta to help her gather herself, but she pushed him away.

She screeched at him, "Don't touch me. She's been living here the whole time I've been gone. Her hair is in the sink and tub. She has pills in the medicine cabinet. I smell her in every room of this place. I smell the smell of sex. The two of you. How could you? She's my sister. Do you hate me so much that you would do this to me? Don't you have …"

Earl yelled over her voice, "Stop it this minute. Anne and I have kept one another company while you've been in the hospital. She has spent most weekends here while you were in the hospital, as she has done since you invited her to stay last June.

166

We missed you and were just keeping one another company while you were gone. I give you my word, Anne and I have not had sex. I have never once kissed her or even held her hand for one second. I swear to you that I'm telling you the truth."

Marta, through gritted teeth, said slowly and deliberately, "I've been in a mental hospital, but I'm not blind or deluded. I know what I see. You don't want to be married to me, you want her. That much I know. The rest of it doesn't matter. She is never to set foot in this place again, ever. Do you hear me? And don't you try to have a slimy rendezvous with her. I will know it if it happens, you can be sure of that."

Marta went to her bedroom and locked the door behind her just as she had the day the paramedic forced open the door and the ambulance took her to the University Medical Center. Earl now realized that something significant had changed since that day. He was no longer worried that she would try to kill herself. He wondered if this was so because he no longer cared if she did. To his surprise, this realization was freeing. The burden with which he had saddled himself for more than three years—the task of keeping alive for himself, and maybe for Marta as well, the illusion that they might one day love one another—was lifted from his shoulders. Along with the lifting of this weight came the stark reality that Marta was his wife and that she was only weeks away from having a baby, their baby, that neither of them wanted. Earl was surprised by the fact that until that moment he had not allowed himself to imagine the baby whose birth was fast approaching, and that he had not given a moment's thought to the question of whether the baby would be a girl or a boy, much less what name to give the baby. He knew Marta well enough to know that she would want no part of naming the baby and that that responsibility was his alone.

The sound of Marta unlocking her door startled Earl, who had not moved a step from where he was standing when Marta had shut the bedroom door behind her. As Marta emerged from her room, Earl saw her as if for the first time. She was a petite woman who at one time had been very pretty, but who had aged far beyond her years. Her features were severe and angular, her eyes dark and unfocused, her skin powder white, the movement of her body neither masculine nor feminine, her clothes purely functional. She looked like a refugee with neither a home that she had left nor a place she was trying to reach, tired by life, and tired of life, carrying in her distended abdomen the weight of something that was not hers, a weight she could barely lift. This was a woman alone in the world, without purpose. She struggled to put on her coat, which was far too small for her. She refused Earl's help. Marta led the way down the stairs and across the campus, this time without visible fear, without perceptible feeling of any sort other than the determination to put one foot in front of the other.

Marta could not forgive Earl for his affair with Anne, which she treated as a fact. She refused to see Earl when he came to visit her in the final two weeks of her hospitalization. On the day of her discharge from the hospital, Earl carried her suitcase as they silently walked to the apartment. She and Earl slept in their own bedrooms, used the kitchen separately, and hardly said a word to each other. Earl was busy with the completion of his honors thesis. That Earl had a life over which she had no control was infuriating to Marta. She suspected that Earl was in touch with Anne, but accused him only with her eyes. In fact, Earl spoke to Anne every day from a pay phone in the student union.

Marta did not leave the apartment except to buy groceries for herself and to see Dr. Anders and the obstetrician. As the due date approached, necessity required that Marta and Earl develop a cordial relationship, which they did. They were polite, even considerate, to one another. Earl told Marta that his mother had offered to stay with them and help out with the baby once it was born. Marta was visibly relieved to hear this, but said nothing. She knew that she would need help in being

168

a mother to the baby and she liked Earl's mother. As Earl had expected, Marta asked him to choose a name for the baby. She also told him that she did not want to know the baby's name until it was born.

Their baby was born a big healthy girl, to whom Earl gave the name Melody. Marta had trouble breastfeeding at first, which was upsetting to her because she felt that the baby wished she had a real mother. Earl's mother unobtrusively helped Marta and Melody to get to know one another. It proved not to be necessary for Earl to tell Marta that they would be moving to the family farm; it was Marta who asked Earl's mother if there was enough room in the farmhouse for her, Earl, and Melody to live there for a little while. Flora said, "Of course there is."

TWELVE

The guests at the funeral reception were staying far longer than Earl had expected, deep into the afternoon, despite the weight of the damp heat in the air. Instead of the grim faces and stooped shoulders that he had anticipated, there was the hum of lively conversation. The presence of old friends, long since moved away—and a glamorous, mysterious stranger who had an uncanny resemblance to Marta—was a rare and welcome event in the life of the people of this farm town, even if it took a funeral to bring it about.

After talking with their grandfather and Leslie, Melody and Warren turned their full attention to the woman who looked like their mother. Melody screwed up her courage to approach her, and Warren strode a single pace behind. As they stood next to her, not yet knowing what to say, she looked even prettier than she had from a distance. She smiled at them in a way that felt genuine and said, "Hello, Melody. Hi, Warren. I'm very sorry about your mother. I miss her too. I'm her sister, Anne."

Melody and Warren each said hello. Melody, not wasting any time, asked, "How do you know our names? How come nobody ever told us about you? Where do you live? Do you have a family?"

171

Anne laughed as she said, "We'll have time for you to ask all of your questions. I live in Chicago and I have a daughter, Sophie, who is the same age as you, Warren. I know your names because your father has told me a lot about you because he's so proud of both of you."

Melody asked again, "How come nobody ever mentioned you, even once?"

"That's a long story, but the gist of it is that your mother and I had a fight before either of you was born, and we stopped talking to one another after it. You know, you think you have all the time in the world until someone you've loved dies. Then you see what a shame it is to have squandered time that you could have spent in a different way with them."

Melody was aware that Anne had sidestepped her question—why no one had ever mentioned her name or even her existence—but she decided to let that go for the moment so as not to be rude. She couldn't stop herself from asking, "How long have you known Daddy?"

"Oh, a very long time. We met when your father and mother were at the university before they got married. I was working in another town at a bakery and went to visit your mother. She was going out with your father, so I met him then. That was about a year before you were born."

"And what about your family?"

"My daughter, Sophie, and I live in an apartment in Chicago. Sophie's in seventh grade. I imagine like you are, Warren."

Warren said, "Yeah."

"Living in an apartment is nothing like living on a farm. You have all this beautiful open space."

"So why do you live in an apartment?" Melody asked.

"Well, I grew up on a farm, like you, and I was always very curious about what there was beyond that little bit of the world. When I was seventeen, I traveled with a friend, hitchhiking and taking buses. I loved the cities we stopped at. You could see movies you'd never see in a small town, and you could talk to lots of different kinds of people, people who you'd be warned to stay away from out here because they're strange and different. I like strange people."

"You saw lots of cities when you were seventeen?"

"Yes, but I was mostly in New York City."

"New York City!" Melody's mind was darting in a hundred directions at the same time. She saw that there would not be time for Anne to answer all of her questions, but the problem wasn't just a matter of time. Asking questions of Anne was frustrating because each time she asked Anne a question, what Anne said didn't really answer the question, and it brought at least a dozen more questions to Melody's mind.

"So what was New York City like?"

"At first, I thought it was a horrible place. The air was filthy, the noise was deafening, nobody looks at anyone else. People just walk by beggars on the street and people sleeping in cardboard boxes as if they were invisible. But I forced myself to get used to it because there are things there that you can't find anywhere else."

"Like what?" Melody shot back.

"For me, it was the music. New York, at that time, was where musicians tried out new music that no one had ever heard before. They experimented with sounds that this part of the country wouldn't hear for years, if ever."

Melody liked Anne already, but could sense that she kept herself just beyond reach. But that was to be expected the first time you talked to someone. Melody persisted because she had been stopped in her tracks every time she had asked her parents about her mother's family or about either of her parents' lives before she was born. Anything from Anne was far better than nothing.

"What was Daddy like when you knew him before I was born?"

"He was the same big and kind man he is now. He loved your mother very much and would do everything he could to make her feel happy and safe."

After her eyes met Warren's knowingly, Melody couldn't resist saying, "He was always doing that right up to when she died."

Keeping the pressure on Anne, Melody asked, "But was he easygoing or shy or what?"

"I wouldn't say he was easygoing. He was intense about everything he did. He took his college courses very seriously, which wasn't considered cool at the time. He wasn't like other college kids—he liked to talk with people about his questions about life."

"Like what?"

"Well, let me see if I can remember. It really wasn't so much that he had specific questions, it was more that he had questions about everything, like what happens to us after we die and why horrible things happen to some people while others are spared, and what it's like to be a girl."

Melody liked the way Anne was now putting her finger on things about her father that she had noticed, but had not been able to put words to. But she also felt sorry for her father because she knew that he had not found anyone with whom to talk to about these things where they lived. Her mother would have hated talk like that. Melody could see that Anne was very smart, but not a showoff. It became increasingly frustrating for Melody that Anne was answering just the parts of the questions that she wanted to answer and was leaving out the parts that Melody most wanted to know about, like whether her father had ever wanted Anne as his girlfriend or his wife.

Warren was hanging on every word that Anne and Melody spoke. He had his own questions, but could not ask them. He wanted to know more about whether his mother had always been so mean, and if she was, how did she get that way, and why did his father marry her. And he also wanted to know if his father had been a football star, and if he was, did everyone look up to him. But Warren did not dare ask Anne those questions and lots of others. He wished he were someone who was not afraid all the time. He wished he were anyone other than who he was. That was something he had never told anyone, even Melody.

Knowing that time would run out, Melody could not decide which questions to ask next. After a few moments' pause, Melody said, "She never mentioned you or anyone else in her family. Who else is there?"

"Our mother and father. They still live in the western part of the state. They used to own a dairy farm, but they're retired now and live in a small house that's just big enough for the two of them. Your grandfather was strict with us. He could be very scary, and your mother and I helped each other as much as we could when he frightened us. Your grandmother was kind-hearted, but I always wished she could have said more of what she was thinking and stood up for us more. I still wish that. And we have a brother who's much older."

"Why didn't they come to the funeral?"

Anne was not in the least frightened or put off by Melody's questions about all that had been kept secret from her. In fact, she admired Melody's courage to vigorously, unapologetically go after what she wanted to know and what she needed to know. Anne was already very fond of Melody.

Anne tried to respond to Melody's question. "I can't answer for anybody but myself, but I think that they didn't want to be reminded of the very hard time we all had being a family together. For a lot of people, putting something out of mind is the best way to get on with life."

"You're here," Melody said, "so you don't think that, do you?"

"I've tried it, but I can't get things to stay out of mind. They keep coming back as if they have a will of their own, so I figure I have no choice but to look them straight in the eye."

175

"Why didn't your husband come with you?"

"When people aren't happy together, it's best for both of them to go their own way, and that's what happened between Sophie's father and me."

"You mean you got divorced?"

Anne could not keep a grin from her face in response to Melody's insistence on dispensing with euphemism.

"That's right. We divorced about ten years ago. He moved to Philadelphia so Sophie and I don't see him much anymore."

"Do you have a job?"

"I do. I'm the assistant manager of a record store. That sounds like more than it is. All it means is that there are two of us who work in the store, and I'm not the manager."

"Do you like doing that job?"

"Yes, it suits me. I love talking to people about music. Customers ask me things like, what's the newest stuff that pop singers are recording?, what's the best album of a group like the Beatles or the Rolling Stones?, where should they start if they want to try out jazz or opera or Beethoven? I enjoy talking with anyone about music, from people who are new to music to people who know a lot more about it than I do."

Melody wondered if Anne was talking to her and Warren in a way that was similar to the way she talked to new customers in the music store. Melody could see that Anne knew how to put people at ease. Maybe it was a knack she had that she used on everyone. Melody didn't want to believe that because she thought that she had finally met a woman she wanted to be like. Anne did not seem fake, but you never know. Melody felt that she was good at knowing who was a fake and who was real. Warren was real. He was incapable of lying or putting on an act.

At that point Earl came over to where they were talking and said, "I'm glad to see that the three of you have had a chance to meet one another."

Melody, seeing that the opportunity for questions was fast disappearing, asked Anne, "How long are you staying?"

"I'm not sure."

It was clear to Melody that her father wanted to talk to Anne by himself. She could see that there was something going on between the two of them that they were trying to keep secret. Melody suspected—and wished—that her father had wanted to marry Anne, but for some reason he couldn't.

Trying to block further questions from Melody, Earl said, "I noticed how long the three of you have been talking, and I'm sure Anne is tired from her trip. So why not let her have a rest and I'll get her another glass of iced tea."

Warren ran over to the tables of iced tea, grabbed a glass, and filled it until it was brimming over. He ran back to Anne with his forearm drenched with iced tea and handed her the glass.

Anne said, "Warren, you're a real gentleman and that's the best way for a guy to be."

Melody was not about to take her father's dismissal without protest. "We'll give her a rest, but we don't want her to leave without saying goodbye and maybe talking to us a little more."

Earl smiled at Melody's fascination with Anne and said, "Move along, your Aunt Anne isn't going anywhere for a while."

Her father seemed to Melody to be solid and self-assured for the first time since her mother had died, and for a long time before that.

Earl and Anne walked into the shade of the cottonwood trees on the east side of the church. They knew they were being closely watched by Melody and Warren as well as by a good many of the remaining guests.

Earl asked, "How was the trip out here?" But before Anne could answer he said, "What a dumb way to greet you after not seeing you for fifteen years."

Anne smiled. "It's funny, it does and it doesn't feel to me like we've been apart for fifteen years because I've been talking to you in my head all this time, but the person I've been talking to hasn't been you, but my invention of you. So I'm having to get used to the fact that you're not the Earl I've been talking to for so long. Even when we spoke on the phone, I've had to imagine you because I couldn't see you.

"It's wonderful to see your face, but I'd love to wrap my two hands around your cheeks like a blind woman who's been talking with someone for fifteen years and just has to feel who they are in more ways than just sound. Don't worry, I won't embarrass you by trying a stunt like that, but that's what I feel like doing. I'm tired of being with your ghost in my head and want to know for sure that I haven't continued to invent you."

Earl said, "That's why I've missed you so much. No one else thinks and talks like you."

"Earl, there are lots of other things I'm afraid you're thinking that are making me nervous talking to you now. Even though we've spent hours on the phone, you haven't actually seen me in the flesh for all these years."

Earl smiled. "You're not alone in being afraid of being seen."

They were silent as they stood looking at one another. Neither Anne nor Earl said that the other did not look any older than when they last saw one another. To have said so would have been to lie. The intervening fifteen years had not been easy on either of them, and time had taken its toll. Anne's face was still beautiful, but it was the face of a woman who had known sorrow and disappointment. There was sadness in her eyes that Earl had not remembered. The skin under her eyes was looser and darker.

Earl's appearance had changed as well. His face was wizened, which made him look considerably older than his years. Where once his thick, blond hair had flopped down heavily over his forehead, his hair was now thin and receding, leaving an expansive pate that shone in the sunlight. His body was no longer the body of a young man growing into the large frame that fate had given him. He was a thinner, less imposing figure now.

Anne broke the silence by saying, "Earl, I can remember exactly where I was standing, and what I was wearing, and how the light in the room looked to me when I picked up the phone and heard your voice when you called a year ago. I don't know if you remember, but you didn't have to say who you were, I knew immediately."

"Of course I remember."

Earl and Anne had talked regularly by phone during most of the year before Marta's death. Randy had been right in thinking that before Marta died, Earl had used public pay phones to make collect calls to Anne. Some were made during the day when Earl was making deliveries or picking up a machine part in town. But there was a risk in making these daytime phone calls—he worried that someone might see him on the phone and wonder why he wasn't calling from the farm or from any of the stores in town where the store owners would have been glad to let him make a call. And if he had been seen more than once making a call on a pay phone, rumors would have begun to fly. So during daylight hours he drove long distances, sometimes twenty miles or more, to find a place where no one knew him. Occasionally he called Anne at night after Grange meetings and the like, but then too, he had to be careful not to be seen using a pay phone, and not to be home too late.

Earl had not known to whom to turn, other than Anne, as he became more and more disturbed by, and unable to put an end to, Marta's increasingly cruel and hateful treatment of Warren. He had seen her go mad before, and so there was no doubt in his mind that she was going mad again. At the same time, Earl was not so self-deceptive as to fail to recognize that, at least in part—maybe entirely—he was again using his problems with Marta as a pretext for calling Anne.

In attempting to work out how to find Anne, Earl knew that Anne's parents would not give him Anne's address or telephone number, so he called the "Best in the Mid-West Bakery" where Anne had worked. The owners, Orin and Ruth Riles, were very fond of Anne, so Earl thought that they would probably have her address, if only to send her a card at Christmas. He knew that Anne had spoken to them about him, so they were familiar with his name. When Earl phoned the bakery, he told Mrs. Riles that Marta was in a difficult predicament and needed Anne's help, so he was trying to get in touch with her. She was glad to give Earl Anne's address and phone number in Chicago and told him to say hello to Anne for her and Orin.

When Earl made the call from a pay phone in a neighboring town, he felt like a ten-year-old doing something secret and forbidden. Anne picked up the phone, and when Earl said, "Hello," the words burst out of her, "Earl, how good to hear from you!'"

So began the year of phone calls between Earl and Anne. In the initial conversation, after Earl called back collect once he had run out of coins, he told Anne that he was at his wits' end concerning how to stop Marta from treating their children—particularly Warren—so cruelly. He said to Anne, in a voice that he hoped did not sound whiny and pathetic, "I assumed that with time Marta would return to being the person she'd been before her breakdown, but I was wrong about that. Marta never recovered from the breakdown she had at State. For the past fourteen years she has simulated sanity successfully enough to fool everyone outside the family. Marta has been so frightened and suspicious that she's been incapable of love or even genuine affection for anyone. She's collapsed into herself the way she did when she had her breakdown at the university. I don't know why I'm telling you all of this. You know it all firsthand: she banished you from her kingdom, and forbade

180

me ever to speak to you again. Melody, Warren, and I have lived with Marta in her insane world."

Earl didn't leave room for a response from Anne. He had been waiting to talk to Anne for fourteen years. He could not stop. "Marta would have been incapable of caring for Melody as a baby had it not been for my mother's help, both during the weeks when my mother lived with us in the attic apartment, and after we moved to the farm. My mother not only helped Marta with the chores involved in raising Melody, she showed her what it meant to be tender with a baby, how to hold her, soothe her, and calm her, and how to play with her and sing to her and talk to her. It was heartbreaking to watch my mother do for Marta what she was also doing for Melody. My mother gave her the tenderness and love and encouragement that she had never received from her own mother. Marta softened during those years. It was the best period in the life of our family. It was the only time I felt a ray of hope for Marta and for our marriage.

"But that didn't last long enough to prepare Marta for what was to come. Even though we were taking precautions, Marta got pregnant again, and that was more than she could take. She didn't want a second child, but neither my mother nor I could convince her to have the pregnancy ended. It was legal at that point to have an abortion and it could have been done safely in a hospital, but she would have none of it. You know how she is.

When Warren was born, she could hardly get herself to hold him. My mother took care of him except for the nursing, which Marta attempted for a few weeks before giving up. She blamed Warren for rejecting her. From then on, my mother gave him his bottle while Marta attended to Melody, who was four when Warren was born. My mother did everything she could to help Marta be gentle with Warren, but nothing seemed to make any difference. I think that his being a boy made it even harder for

Marta. My hopes for Marta and our family died as I watched what was happening between Marta and Warren.

"My father's arthritis was getting worse and it became impossible for him to do anything but supervise the hired hands. My mother didn't want to leave Marta alone with the children, but it became harder and harder for my father to climb the stairs to the second floor of the house. When Warren was two and Melody six, my parents moved to North Carolina to live near Leslie and her family. Marta found my mother's leaving as hard as it was for Melody and Warren, although she never said a word about it. She took to bed for a week when my parents left. When she finally got out of bed, she was furious at all of us. Even the affection that she had once been able to show Melody dried up, though she was never as harsh with Melody as she was with Warren."

Anne found it painful to listen to Earl's account of what he, Marta, and the children had been through all these years. At the same time, though she was ashamed to admit it to herself, she also felt surprised, relieved—in truth, overjoyed—by the fact that Earl had called her and that she was talking with him once again after fourteen years of silence. Was she glad to hear that Earl and Marta's life together had been disastrous? Yes and no, but mostly yes was the truth, she thought. Was she glad that Earl was turning to her when he could take it no longer with Marta? No question about it.

Earl finally stopped and said, "I've been going on for most of an hour without giving you a chance to say anything. I haven't even asked you how you've been for the past fourteen years."

Anne said, "I've often thought of you and Marta and have wondered how both of you are, so I'm glad that you've called and have told me something of what's happened. And it's been good to have a chance to listen to your voice for an hour."

Anne could hear how formal her speech had become. She knew she was trying to hide her excitement, and was erring in the opposite direction.

After a few weeks, the phone calls became a lifeline for both Earl and Anne. They never lacked for something to talk about, and the time that they had to talk always seemed far too short. On one gray early autumn afternoon, Earl chose to drive quite a distance to use a pay phone. On the way, he was lost in thought. He felt ashamed that he had not had the courage to say goodbye to Anne in person after Marta forbade him from ever seeing her again. He had called her and explained, but that's not the same as actually having had the courage to go and see her one last time.

The phone calls to this point had been filled mostly with stories of Earl's life since returning to the farm. Earl, for the first time, tried to imagine how Anne had taken the abrupt end of the life he and she had led while Marta was in the hospital. To think she was heartbroken was to give himself too much importance to her, but at the very least she must have felt directionless.

When Earl spotted a pay phone at a filling station, he filled the pickup with gas to justify his use of the phone. When Anne answered and they'd said their hellos, Earl told Anne that he'd been trying to imagine what it had been like for her after Marta decreed the end of the life the three of them had had together.

Anne said, "I'm afraid the answer to your question isn't a very interesting one." She told Earl about having moved to Chicago. She'd gone to night school, graduated, and after a series of temp jobs eventually found a position as an assistant to the administrative director of the Ballet.

"I did things, but I was hardly present in my own life. I had no appetite for anything. The world was colorless. I mean that literally. I thought for a while that I was becoming color blind.

"I married a man I met at night school. We'd known each other less than a year. It sounds strange, but it felt as if he married me, but I didn't marry him. Of course, we had a child—everybody did—but he didn't like the day-to-day business of raising a child. That, plus my brief affair, did us in. After the divorce was final, it was as if nothing had changed. I didn't miss him. I hardly noticed his absence. I don't think I ever knew him or that he ever knew me.

"There is one thing on the positive side of the ledger. I am proud of the way I'm able to be a good mother for Sophie. You can't imagine the joy I feel when I see her laugh and the pain I feel when I let her down. I don't think anyone can understand who I am unless they understand that about me."

Anne and Earl were well aware that she hadn't answered the question he was really asking: how had she felt when the life they'd lived together while Marta was in the hospital came to a crashing end. In this and their other phone calls, neither Earl nor Anne said a word about their feelings for one another. Both of them knew, as they had at State, that they did not have it in them to collude in Earl's secretly arranging to leave Marta with two children or to leave her and take the children with him.

* * *

Though Earl had led something of a double life for the year leading up to Marta's death, he had not betrayed Marta or made plans to leave her, he told himself. He found Randy's behavior in connection with Marta's death to be puzzlingly mean-spirited, even vengeful. As far as Earl knew, he had never done anything hurtful to Randy.

In dealing with Randy, Earl was as clear as he had ever been in his life about anything. First, he would never acknowledge to anyone that Marta had attempted to put a knife through Warren's hand. This was nobody's business. Second, neither Warren nor Melody needed to be protected from Marta any longer, so questions regarding her treatment of them served no purpose. And third, Earl was not the least bit frightened by Randy's insinuations that people might "get the wrong idea" about his account of Marta's death, by which he knew Randy meant that people would think he had intentionally killed Marta for sleazy reasons that he was keeping secret. Earl didn't give a damn what people gossiped about. His friends would remain his friends, and those who didn't know him or didn't like him were welcome to think whatever they wanted.

While Randy's insinuations were irritants that Earl resented, his self-accusations had become a real torment. At the end of the day on which Marta was killed, after Melody and Warren were asleep in their room, Earl spoke with Anne for more than two hours. This conversation was different from any that they had previously had because Earl was more honest with himself and with Anne than he had ever been.

He said to her, "I ask myself, over and over, did I hit her as hard as I did because I wanted to kill her? The answer to that question that feels most honest to me is, I don't know. What I do know is that I'm not sorry she's dead. But I don't feel that I had the right to kill her. No one has that right. If I wanted to be rid of her, I should have divorced her, but I didn't have what it would have taken to do that. Killing her intentionally, if that's what I did, was a coward's way out."

Anne listened for a long time as Earl went round and round in circles. She finally said, "Earl, you'll never know whether or not you tried to kill her. No one really knows why they do anything they do—that's not the way we know ourselves. We can't explain ourselves, even to ourselves. We make up reasons afterwards, and it all seems to fit together, but we're fooling ourselves if we think that we've explained why we did what we did."

"Since Marta died this morning, my mind has been racing. I can't seem to focus."

"When I was growing up," Anne said, "there were months, probably years at a time, when I didn't understand much of what people were saying or what I was thinking. I learned to pick up enough cues to get the gist of what was expected of me. I could behave as I was supposed to behave most of the time.

What frightened me most was being found out and locked up in a mental hospital."

"You never told me that it was that bad."

"You have no idea how ashamed I felt then, and feel now. Who would want to be around someone as crazy as I am? I'm afraid you won't."

Given the number of phone conversations Anne and Earl had had that year, neither could say exactly when a particular thing had been said, or sometimes, which of them had said it—with the exception of this conversation.

Toward the end of the phone call, Anne said, "This may sound selfish to you, and if it does, I want you to tell me, but I wonder if it would be all right with you if I attend Marta's funeral?"

Her request was followed by a long silence. As she waited for Earl's response, Anne was afraid that once again she had failed to understand what was happening between her and a man, and she had said something she shouldn't have. She had been lonely for a long time and had wanted to see Earl, she knew that. But what she hoped would happen with him was a mystery to her. She didn't know if she wanted to marry him. She thought that that's what she wanted. But how could she know before seeing if he was the least bit interested in her as a real person as opposed to a voice on a telephone line in an imaginary relationship in which they had no responsibility at all for one another, much less for each other's children. In a teen-age romantic daydream, they would meet at the funeral, fall in love, have babies, and raise a family together. But she never much believed in that sort of daydream, even as a teenager.

Standing under the cottonwood trees, talking face to face for the first time since college, now thirty-four and thirty-seven years old, they were no longer the same people they had been when Anne was banished by Marta. In a way, everything was different now: Marta was dead, and Earl was now a widower; Earl, Melody, and Warren would never again have to face

Marta's insane cruelty; Anne lived and worked in Chicago with her eleven-year-old daughter; Earl owned and ran the family farm and had given up any idea of becoming an engineer or anything other than a farmer.

And yet, everything was the same as it always had been: Earl was Earl and Anne was Anne. Earl was drawn to Anne as strongly as he had ever been—she was the sexiest, most beautiful, most intelligent woman he had ever met, and to his surprise and bewilderment, she seemed interested in him. He was prepared, as always, to accept her for who she was, including the fact that she was a perennial liar—or if one were to put it more charitably, she was a perennial storyteller, preserving essential truths and conveying them in disguised form.

And Anne was still Anne. What she felt for Earl was something she had never felt for any other man, though she did not have words to say what that was. When Marta was alive, Anne didn't like to call it love. Even now, after Marta's death, she did not know if love was the right word for what she felt. She had a hard time believing anything she felt, but she was quite sure that she had felt more nervous and more excited about meeting Earl at the funeral than she could remember ever feeling. That must mean that he mattered more than most anything or anyone had ever mattered to her, except Sophie. At least she hoped it did.

The last guests at the reception were still gathered in groups of three or four, even though the evening was encroaching on the afternoon. The tables that once held the freshly cut flowers, the clear glass pitchers of iced tea sweating in the August heat, and the sandwiches from the diner now looked tired, with their flowers wilted, the pitchers empty except for the bloated lemon slices piled at their base and the half-eaten food enveloped in napkins. Long shadows draped the front of the church, darkening its bright white paint to the soft, gray-brown color of quail. The air was beginning to stir as the sun, now a dark orange, seemed to be preparing to rest for the night.

THIRTEEN

Melody and Warren kept an eye on Anne all afternoon. They scrutinized the way she handled the other guests as they introduced themselves to her. Melody, completely enthralled with Anne, said to Warren, "I can't believe that she's our mother's sister, and that she's related to us. It's as if a hummingbird were born to a family of lizards. I've never seen anyone so beautiful except in the movies. That's how I'd like to be, not like all the other women here."

Warren, interrupting Melody, said, "I don't like her. It's all an act. Why can't you see that? You don't mean anything to her. Nobody means anything to her except herself. We're an audience for her performance. We don't mean any more to her than we do to movie stars we see on television. They don't even know we exist."

"Warren, stop that. You don't know what you're talking about."

"And you do?"

"I know more about people than you do," Melody insisted.

"You do? Is that why you knew how to play our mother better than I did?"

The bitterness in Warren's voice stung Melody.

"I didn't play her better than you, she had it in for you more than she did for me. I never knew why."

"I don't care why. She's dead, really dead. I never gave in to her. There's only one of us left and it's me. I won. You have to admit that," Warren said, glaring at Melody.

"No one won."

"I did and I'm glad I did. I'm the reason she's dead."

"Daddy killed her. You didn't lay a hand on her." Melody regretted having used the word "hand." The word made her think of the hand Warren used to suck his thumb, the hand that had driven their mother crazy.

"You know I killed her," Warren insisted. "She'd be alive now if it weren't for me, and I'm glad that she's dead. If she were alive, you would never have met your movie star from Chicago. You wouldn't have had the fun of ogling at her the way you do. She has you eating out of the palm of her hand like a rabbit or a horse."

Melody had never seen Warren like this. Scathing words were pouring out of him. He was impenetrable. She felt that she was on her own now, as was he, for the first time. Melody was frightened, not in the way she had been frightened of her mother, but in the way she was frightened by the idea of her father dying.

Melody began talking, but did not know what would come out of her mouth. She rambled pleadingly, "I wasn't eating out of her hand. Talking with her is like seeing a movie. I like a lot of movies. You do too. Usually we like the same movies, but sometimes we don't. Once in a while I like one that's made more for girls and you like one that's made more for boys. Aunt Anne is like a movie that's made for girls. The way she looks so beautiful in her elegant dress and the way she talks and gets everyone curious about her by keeping herself aloof and mysterious—all that is acting meant for the girls and women. I liked it, but I didn't believe it was true."

Warren now spit out his words. "I hate her. She has no business being here. *She* wouldn't talk to her sister and didn't want to see her ever again. I can see why. She's worse than *her*. At least *she* wasn't acting all the time, she was exactly who she seemed to be—a horrible person. This woman is like a traveling circus. We're all supposed to fall to our knees and bow to her. Tomorrow she'll be gone and everyone will be talking about her. You and Earl will be wishing she were still here. But both of you are morons if you can't see through her. If she stayed for more than a day, she wouldn't know what to do. She wouldn't stay because we're not good enough for her. We're like a freak show for her. You are. Daddy is. I am. I'm the worst freak in her book. She feels she's so beautiful in her fancy dress. I don't understand all the talk about dresses. What does it matter? It's disgusting to see you fall all over yourself for her. I don't know who you are when you do that. I'm not surprised that Earl fawns over her. He can't stand up to women. He was our mother's slave, but you? I expected more of you. I did. I expected you'd see through her." Warren was trembling as he spoke.

Melody thought that Warren was ashamed and furious at himself for having been taken in by Anne and that for a moment he had hoped she would change his life, change the life of the whole family. She had had the same hope. She had almost asked Anne if she and her father were going to get married. She knew Warren felt duped, he felt like a fool. Anne had hurt him in one of the few ways their mother had never hurt him. He was caught offguard. But she knew there was more to it than that.

Warren watched the toe of his shoe make lines in the dry dirt. Melody tried to look into his eyes, but he refused to let her. Beside herself, not knowing what to do, Melody began to cry. She felt the agony that Warren had stored up somewhere in him over the course of his life. Melody could see that she had not succeeded in sparing Warren the full force of their mother's hatred and their father's cowardice. It had all gotten through to Warren. Melody had tried to be more than a sister to Warren, she had tried to be a mother to him. She now saw that she had failed.

This was the first time that Warren had seen Melody cry. Warren had never once cried even when, as a very young child, his mother told him again and again that she hated him and wished he had never been born or when she hit him with a belt or locked him in the closet. Melody knew that Warren would never cry. To cry would be to admit that the pain he had experienced had taken him over and was now part of him. Even though their mother was the one who had died, he had not won at all—she was as powerful in death as she had been in life. Melody could see at that moment that Warren would never grow up, he would never leave home, he would never make a life of his own. He might grow bigger, but that is not the same as growing up. He might live in a different place, but that is not the same as leaving home. He might find a job, and even marry—though she doubted he would marry—but that is not the same as his making a life of his own.

Melody leaned her back against the side of the church, slid down to the ground, and sat there crying with her head on her knees and her hands clasping her skirt, which was tented over her knees and shins. She thought she had felt her dress tear in back as she slid down the wall of the church.

Warren sat down next to her and said, "I'm sorry I made you cry."

Melody said, "It's about time one of us cried."

Warren was silent for a little while before saying, "There's no use in crying. It won't change anything."

Melody and Warren sat there silently side by side for a long time. One of the guests, the wife of a neighboring farmer, saw Melody and Warren sitting solemnly with their backs against the side of the church. She came over and said, "This is a very sad day for your family and for the rest of us. Your mother was a wonderful person."

Melody and Warren nodded.

Earl took care of getting everyone squared away for the night—his father and Leslie at the Wilkins' house, and Anne at the house of a widow in town who rented out rooms, but said she would not accept a penny from Anne. For Melody and Warren, it seemed to take forever for their father to say good-bye to their grandfather, Leslie, and Anne. The three of them would be leaving for home early the next morning.

Earl, Melody, and Warren shared the front seat of the pickup as they drove back to the farm. They all were too tired to talk. By the time they got home it was after nine. Earl fed and watered the horses. Melody and Warren brushed their teeth and got into bed, too tired to talk.

The next morning Melody was awakened abruptly by her father's heavy footsteps on the stairs. She knew something was the matter and saw that Warren was not in his bed. Earl knocked softly on the door before opening it. Melody sat up and looked at her father expectantly. His face was ashen and creased with pain. He walked halfway into the room and stopped. Awkwardly, he sat down at the end of Melody's bed. He tried to speak, but it seemed that there wasn't enough air in his lungs with which to squeeze out the words he was trying to say. After several attempts at speaking, he said in a quiet, thin voice, "Melody, something terrible has happened. Warren hung himself in the barn last night. I found him this morning."

Melody tried to convince herself that she was dreaming, but couldn't. Nonetheless, she persisted in trying to wake herself up from the nightmare. As she settled into the reality of what her father had said, she felt empty, hollowed out, no longer the person she had been. She was now alone in a world she no longer wanted to live in. Neither she nor her father said anything. Melody, turning to Warren's vacant bed, noticed a folded piece of notebook paper on the table between their beds. She unfolded it and read it to herself several times.

> Dear Melody,
>
> I'm not at all scared for the first time in my life. I have had enough of living. I dread everything that will happen from here on if I continue to live, so I'm glad that I won't have to live it. You are the only good thing that happened to me in my whole life. I would hate to feel that I'm holding you back because you want to take care of me. I'm not made for this life and you are.
>
> Warren
>
> P. S. I'm sorry I made you cry yesterday.

Tears rolled down Melody's face as she read the letter. She re-folded it and tucked it under the sheets. Choking on her tears, she said to her father, a few words at a time, "He said … he felt relieved … not to have to live any longer … He said he wasn't scared … He said goodbye … to both of us."

When Melody looked up at her father, his face was wet with tears. He said, "I want to get Warren out of the barn and onto his bed and I don't want you to see him until he's on his bed, so please go out back while I do that."

An hour earlier, when Earl discovered Warren's body in the barn hanging from a rope tied to a beam at the edge of the loft, he pulled Warren's body up into the loft, untied the knot in the rope, and laid him down on the straw. He sat next to Warren for some time before walking back to the house to tell Melody what had happened.

On returning to the barn after talking to Melody, Earl climbed the wooden ladder to the loft where Warren was laying. On his knees, Earl carefully slid his hands and forearms under Warren's neck and knees before lifting the outstretched body. Earl awkwardly carried the body down the ladder from the loft. The logistics of this maneuver were a welcome distraction from the fact of his son's suicide. After Earl carried Warren back to the house, he gently placed him on Melody's bed so he could straighten up the sheets and blankets on Warren's bed before placing him on top of the blankets and sliding the pillow under his head.

Earl stood at the side of Warren's bed looking down at him. As he stood there, Earl recalled the expression on Warren's face when, as so often happened, Marta called him to go out back with her for a scolding or a beating or to put ointment on his thumbs or gloves on his hands. Warren's face never betrayed his fear, if indeed that was what he was feeling. Warren seemed to be preparing himself to endure whatever Marta had in store for him without giving her the satisfaction of thinking she had broken him. Earl felt a crushing indictment of himself for having failed so thoroughly to protect his son. He could feel his own mother looking at him with profound disappointment in her eyes. She would have held herself responsible for having raised a child capable of standing by while his own son was being tortured every day of his life. "Tortured" was the right word if he was to be honest with himself, Earl thought. If he could have another chance, he would stand up to Marta. But there were no more chances. Both Marta and Warren were dead—only five days separating their deaths. Both deaths, Earl thought, were his doing. He felt that he had killed Marta in order to release Warren from her cruelty, and to redeem himself for having failed Warren and Melody so abysmally. But he had not felt redeemed after killing Marta—he'd felt even more guilty of cowardice. He had not been able to stand up to Marta while she was alive; he could only stand up to her for a moment before she died.

Earl knelt down by the side of Warren's bed, took the boy's cold hand in his, and said, "I'm sorry I wasn't a better father to you."

Earl left the room and gathered some towels, a bucket of warm water, and a bar of soap. On returning to the children's bedroom, he rolled Warren's body to one side and placed a towel under him and then centered Warren on the towel. After taking off all of Warren's clothes, Earl removed pieces of hay from Warren's hair as a mother might tidy up a small child who has played in a field. With the edge of one of the towels soaked with soapy water, Earl carefully and tenderly washed the dirt from Warren's face. The rope had left deep abrasions flecked with blood on the front of the boy's neck, which were not visible when Earl lifted Warren's head and positioned it on the pillow. Earl then took Warren's small hands in his, one at a time, and washed them until they were clean and then dried them with a new towel. Earl, in a daze, moved systematically down the torso to the legs and feet, and then turned Warren on his side to wash his back and buttocks.

Earl wept as he dressed Warren in fresh clothes. He was reminded of coming back to the house after the family had spent an afternoon at a neighbor's farm. Earl's parents were still living with them. He remembered carrying Warren up the stairs to his bed and pulling one of Warren's little arms, and then the other, through the sleeves of his pajamas while the small boy was fast asleep. He had loved Warren deeply. So why had he not protected him better? Even as a small boy, Warren had been alone as he faced the world. No, Earl corrected himself, it was not true that Warren had been alone. Melody had loved him and protected him, so far as she could. Why, he asked himself, had he not done for Warren what Melody had done? Earl had a thousand responses to the question, but at that moment, only one occurred to him: he had been loyal to Marta, even when that loyalty had involved betraying his children, his parents, and himself. What sick kind of loyalty is that? Loyalty to whom, to what, for what?

Something snapped inside Earl at that moment. It was as if he had shouted, "Stop!" at the top of his lungs. He hated himself for finding comfort in his self-excoriations. He was holding his dead son's right ankle trying to pull the sock onto the foot. Self-laceration was far easier than being present in the reality of what he was actually doing at that moment. It was a walk in the park, as his father would have put it.

Earl stood and leaned down to brush a few strands of Warren's hair back from his forehead before he went out back to get Melody. She was sitting on a broken kitchen chair in the morning sun, looking out into the partially harvested wheat fields. It was strange to see her without Warren next to her. Earl walked to where she was sitting and stood by her looking out at the wheat as if he were trying to catch a glimpse of whatever it was out there that she was looking at so intently. He wanted to say something, but he didn't know what.

ABOUT THE AUTHOR

Thomas Ogden, MD, has published eleven books of essays on the theory and practice of psychoanalysis and on the writings of Frost, Borges, Kafka, Heaney, Stevens, and others. His most recent books include *The Analyst's Ear and the Critic's Eye: Rethinking Psychoanalysis and Literature* (coauthored with B. Ogden); *Creative Readings: Essays on Seminal Analytic Works*; *Rediscovering Psychoanalysis: Thinking and Dreaming, Learning and Forgetting*; and *This Art of Psychoanalysis: Dreaming Undreamt Dreams and Interrupted Cries*. His work has been translated into nineteen languages.

Dr. Ogden was awarded the 2004 *International Journal of Psychoanalysis* Award for "The Most Important Paper of the Year"; the 2010 Haskell Norman Prize for "outstanding achievement as a psychoanalytic clinician, teacher, and theoretician"; and the 2012 Sigourney Award for his "contributions to the field of psychoanalysis." He practices psychoanalysis and teaches both psychoanalysis and creative writing in San Francisco.